Step-Chain

All over the country children go to stay with step-parents, stepbrothers and stepsisters at the weekends. It's just like an endless chain. A step-chain. *Too Good To Be True* is the fourth link in this step-chain.

I'm Becca. Mum and I have been by ourselves for a while, but now Mum has a boyfriend. I'm pleased she's happy with Patrick. There's just one problem: she wants me to meet his daughter, Lissie. I wouldn't mind except that Mum makes out that Lissie is perfect in every way. How can I compete with that?

Collect the links in the step-chain! You never know who you'll meet on the way...

Step-Chain

TOO GOOD TO BE TRUE

Ann Bryant

mammoth

First published in Great Britain 2001
by Egmont Books Limited
239 Kensington High Street
London W8 6SA

Copyright © 2001 Ann Bryant
Series conceived and created by Ann Bryant
Cover illustration copyright © 2001 Mark Oliver

The moral rights of the author and cover illustrator have
been asserted

Series editor: Anne Finnis

ISBN 0 7497 4325 5

3 5 7 9 10 8 6 4 2

Typeset by Avon Dataset Ltd, Bidford on Avon, B50 4JH
(www.avondataset.co.uk)
Printed and bound in Great Britain by
Cox & Wyman Ltd, Reading, Berkshire

CONTENTS

Step-Chain

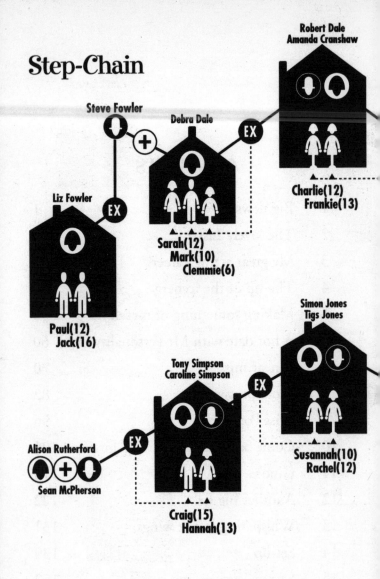

Robert Dale
Amanda Cranshaw

Charlie(12)
Frankie(13)

Steve Fowler

Debra Dale

EX

Sarah(12)
Mark(10)
Clemmie(6)

Liz Fowler

EX

Paul(12)
Jack(16)

Simon Jones
Tigs Jones

Susannah(10)
Rachel(12)

Tony Simpson
Caroline Simpson

EX

Alison Rutherford

Sean McPherson

EX

Craig(15)
Hannah(13)

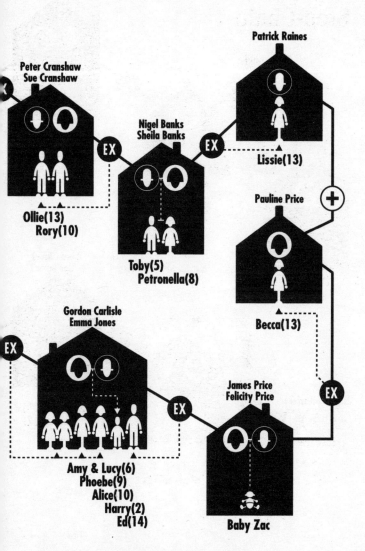

Read on to discover all the links . . .

1 BIG NEWS

I should have known this was going to be a bad day from the moment I got out of bed and squinted at myself in the mirror. There, shining like a beacon in the very middle of my chin, was the biggest spot I think I've ever seen on anyone. It made the other few spots on my face look like the tiniest of freckles. I rootled around on my dressing-table, desperately searching for some spot cream, then I pulled the dressing-table away from the wall to see if it had fallen down the back. Big mistake! All I succeeded in doing was making the pots and sticks, jars and bottles go sliding off the front.

It was too dark for me to see down the back, and I couldn't lug the thing any further away from the wall because my hairbrush was wedged underneath it at the front, so I crouched down and tried to squeeze myself between the dressing-table and the wall. And – guess what? – my head got stuck.

'You stupid, pathetic thing!' I screeched at the dressing-table. And then I heard Mum's voice come floating up from the kitchen. I couldn't make out what she was saying because one of my ears was pressed against the wall and the other against the back of the dressing-table. And that just made me even madder.

Next thing, I heard her voice right behind me.

'Oh Becky, you do look funny!' she spluttered through her giggles. 'Sorry to laugh, love . . . Are you all right?'

'No, I am *not* all right,' I snapped.

'Here, let me help.'

Mum must have unwedged my hairbrush, because the dressing-table suddenly moved with a big jolt about ten centimetres, and I managed to get my head out. She was still trying not to laugh, which made me want to kill her.

'Did you drop something down there?' she asked, struggling to keep a serious look on her face.

'No, Mum, I'm just doing my head-squeezing exercise –' That made her really crease up – 'and stop staring at me.'

I saw her purse her lips to try to stop herself laughing before she went out. I really didn't know what was so funny. . . until I looked in the mirror.

'Oh great!'

My ears were bright red, I'd got dust round one side of my face and a furry grey cobweb in my fringe. Didn't Mum *ever* clean behind furniture?

Mum didn't look at me when I went down for breakfast. I'd put make-up on the spot so it didn't shine so much, it just looked crusty and a bit brown. I'd done what I could with my hair, but I'm in the middle of growing it so it's not really got a style. It kind of hangs around my face in strange-looking clumps. There was no way I could make my actual body look nice because our school uniform must have been designed by a ninety-year-old man who's colour blind and hates girls.

'Do you want me to try and do something with that spot?' Mum asked in her gentlest voice.

'You're not squeezing it, Mum.'

'I've no intention of squeezing it. I was going to re-apply the make-up, that's all.'

So she did, and I had to admit, it looked a whole lot better when she'd finished.

'We'll have a take-away tonight, shall we?' she went on brightly.

I stopped in the middle of stuffing my packed

lunch in my school bag. You see, I know my mum, and I knew for sure and certain that the take-away wasn't the only thing on her agenda. No – she had something important that she wanted to talk to me about. Her voice was too bright. She didn't fool me for a minute.

'Why? What have you got to tell me?' I asked, narrowing my eyes.

'Well, we'll talk later, shall we . . . over the take-away?'

'*She's* nice,' said Tanya, jabbing the glossy page with her finger.

'She's *lovely*!'

'*She's* wearing those trousers my sister wants . . .'

'You're very quiet, Bex,' commented Louise.

'Mmm.'

I've tried hard to train people to call me Becca, but no one takes any notice of me. It's always Becky from Mum, Gran and my teachers, and Bex from my friends.

'Is something wrong?' asked Maddy.

'Probably not.'

I picked up a piece of my hair and inspected it for split ends. Even without looking at them I knew I'd got them interested.

'Oh come on, stop being mysterious, Bex,' said Tanya. 'We're all dying to know what's up now.'

They all leaned forward as though I was about to let them in on something juicy I'd found out about one of the teachers or something.

'You know Mum . . .'

'Yeah, she's got that boyfriend, hasn't she?'

'And they've just got back from Portugal, haven't they?'

'She's not dumped him, has she?'

'Omigod!' screeched Maddy. 'Don't say *he's* dumped *her*! That's it, isn't it, Bex?'

'Or are they getting married or something?' squeaked Tanya.

'Yeah, and he's got a job as a missionary in Africa and you've got to go and live in a mud hut . . .' Louise finished off, eyes wide.

'Look, do you want to know, or what?' I said in my best nanny's voice to shut them up.

'Yeah . . . sorry.'

They waited, all big-eyed and excited, and I suddenly realised I didn't actually have anything to tell them. I mean, they weren't going to be too impressed with the truth . . .

Mum's going to talk to me this evening.

What about?

Dunno.

I had to say it though. They were all waiting breathlessly.

'Well, you know Mum . . .' I was speaking really slowly, desperately hoping that I might suddenly think of a way of making my great non-event sound like something stunningly mysterious. It was no good. I'd just have to say it. 'Well, she wants to talk to me about

7

something and I don't know what it is . . .'

Tanya looked puzzled. 'So what makes you think it might be something important?'

'Just a feeling,' I said, trying to look mysterious.

Louise giggled. 'You do look funny when you squint like that, Bex.'

(That's the last time I'd try to look mysterious.)

Maddy put her arm round me. 'Don't be horrible, Lou. Bex might be about to have a baby sister or something – you never know.'

'Cool!' said Tanya.

Then they all went back to the magazine. Just like that! Leaving me with my jaw dropped open, contemplating a baby sister or brother.

While Mum was picking up the take-away that evening, and I was at home getting plates and knives and forks out, I started daydreaming.

What did your mum say, Bex?

Oh, nothing much – just that when she was in

Portugal she bought a lottery ticket and she won, so we're buying a villa out there . . . Yeah, cool, isn't it? Mum's just picking up the Porsche at the moment . . . What? No, she's given up work for ever . . . Sorry, can't make it after school – we're popping over to Paris for dinner . . .

I was so deep in my dream, I didn't hear Mum coming in.

A couple of minutes later we were tucking into Chicken Korma and all the trimmings. Mum was blinking rapidly. (She always does that when she's concentrating or nervous.) The moment had come.

'You haven't got any sleepovers or anything planned for Saturday evening, have you?' she began, her eyes on the Korma, her voice trying to sound casual (which wasn't working).

My heartbeat went up a bit. 'No . . .'

'Only I was going to invite Patrick over . . .'

So? Nothing unusual about that.

'Uh-huh . . .'

'And there's someone he wants you to meet . . .'

My heart rate doubled. And my mind went into overdrive. *Patrick was gay. He was bringing his partner along. Mum isn't going out with Patrick at all. I'd got it all wrong.* What would my friends make of *this*?

'. . . and *she* wants to meet *you* too,' Mum went on, smiling shakily.

She?

'Who?'

'Patrick's daughter, Lissie. She's thirteen, just like you.'

2 THE LOVELY LISSIE

'What!' It had come out like a squeak I was so
gobsmacked. 'Why didn't you tell me Patrick
had got a daughter?'

Mum started gabbling. 'Patrick didn't tell
Lissie about you either. It's just that we wanted
to be quite sure about one another before
introducing you two to each other. It could be
awkward and hurtful if you got to know each
other, and then Patrick and I split up.'

I wasn't really listening to Mum's answer. I
was too busy imagining what Maddy and the
others would say about *this*! I mean, wow!

They were going to be so impressed.

'So she'll be like a kind of . . . stepsister?' I managed to utter.

Mum laughed happily. 'I suppose so, yes!'

'So what does she look like? Is she like me?'

'She's a positive sweetie. Very sensitive and bright – lovely looking. I'm sure you'll get on fine.'

I felt as though someone had come along and vacuumed all my spit out. Lissie was clearly a big hit with Mum. She was clever *and* good looking. How could I compete with that? I gulped some water and waited but Mum seemed to have finished. I couldn't believe it. There was so much more I needed to know.

Like . . . *Is she tall, short, slim, thin, trendy, sporty, brown eyes, blue eyes, long hair, short hair, dark hair, fair hair, straight hair, curly hair, highlights, piercings, tattoos . . .?*

'Don't look so worried, Becky. She's just another thirteen-year-old.'

'What, like me?' I asked hopefully.

'Well . . . yes, I suppose so . . .'

Well . . . yes, I suppose so . . . What did that mean? Why all the hesitation? I took another drink of water.

'Just tell me what she's like, Mum.'

'I've told you, she's very nice . . . and she's really into music.'

'What? Pop music?'

'Not exactly, no. More . . . classical music. She plays the cello, you see.'

I pushed my plate away slowly. 'I expect she's really good at it, isn't she?' I asked, dreading the answer.

'I . . . er . . . pretty good, yes. I've only heard her play once – in her room. And it sounded – yes – very good.'

Oh God, I can't take much more! But there was still the most important question to be answered. *OK, take a deep breath, Becca . . .*

'What exactly does she look like?'

13

'Er . . . let me see . . . shoulder-length hair, like you . . .' Mum broke off to give me a big beam. I felt about six and a half. It was like she was trying to reassure me. Which meant that Lissie must really be something wonderful.

'Dark or fair?' I snapped.

'Dark . . . with a lovely sheen to it.'

It would *have*.

'Straight or curly?'

'Straight.'

'And is she really cool? What clothes does she wear?'

Mum laughed in this giggly way that she'd never done before. 'I don't know about cool. She just wears jeans and tops like you.'

I was right! Lissie was sounding wonderful and Mum had clicked that I wasn't too happy, so she was playing it down. I bet Lissie had beautiful, clear, spot-free skin. She probably did modelling for soap or shampoo or something. My hair was going to look like clumps of dead weeds next to her straight dark shiny hair. And as for my face – well, that would look like pimple city. What on earth was she going to think when she met me on Saturday evening? *Saturday evening!* That was three days away! Something had to be done to stop this before it went any further.

'Oh no!' I clapped my hand to my forehead.

'What?' Mum sat up, looking concerned.

'I've just remembered Tanya asked me to go round to her place on Saturday. Her parents are having a dinner party and Tanya's got nothing to do . . .'

'That's OK, we can make it Friday. Patrick said either day would be fine.'

My brain went into overdrive trying to think of a good reason why Friday was another big no-no, but I couldn't come up with a single thing.

Mum got up from the table and come round to my side. She put her arm round me and gave me a hug.

'There's absolutely nothing to worry about. You don't have to be best mates the moment you set eyes on each other. Just look on it as a nice evening with a couple of friends.'

But I couldn't. I was terrified. I went up to my room and lay on my bed staring at the ceiling. Then I found myself looking down my body at my flat chest. That panicked me even more. What was the betting that Lissie had got boobs? She'd got everything else.

I launched myself off my bed and belted to the top of the stairs. 'Has Lissie got . . .' *What am I doing? I can't ask Mum that!*

'Got what?' Mum called up.

'Got . . . a cello teacher? Or does she teach herself?'

'She's got a teacher. Patrick says she has an hour's lesson every week. Then she practises at home every day up in her room.'

OK, Mum. I'm not writing an essay on the subject.

I slunk back into my room and flopped on to my bed again. Lissie must be mega good on the cello if she had a whole hour's lesson. Anyone I've ever met only has half-hour music lessons. And what was I good at? Sport? No. School work? Definitely no. A musical instrument? No way. Dancing? Not particularly. I racked my brains to think of everything I'd ever done in my life. Surely I was good at something? The effort of coming up with one little personal talent nearly killed me, but I reckoned I could just about say I was OK at acting. I played the part of one of the ugly sisters in the school's pantomime of *Cinderella* at Christmas, and after the performance someone's dad came up to me and said, 'I don't think I've ever laughed so much in all my life. You were terrific. You ought to take it up, you know.'

That compliment lasted me weeks, and I started to dream about being a professional actress, being on telly, and people wanting my autograph. Then when the article all about the panto went in the newspaper there was a photo of Cinderella and the wicked stepmother, but I didn't even get a mention, let alone a photo. So I decided that the man must have been mixing me up with the wicked stepmother when he gave me that compliment. He was quite old so he was probably someone's grandad and couldn't see all that well.

Right now, it seemed like an evil joke that I'd been cast as the ugly stepsister. It was as if the pantomime had been a trial run, and now I was in for the real thing.

Which reminded me – spots, hair and lack of boobs! I lunged at my dressing-table and rubbed spot cream hard into five places on my face, making sure I left a big dollop on top of the chin spot. Then I grabbed my hairbrush and laid into my clumpy hair. No luck there. Next I took my top off and stuck my chest out to see if anything had happened in the last five minutes. Another big disappointment.

I sat down heavily, feeling gutted. And ever so slowly, the feeling turned to anger.

Why *should* I have to meet the great Lissie? Just because Mum's fallen in love with some man or other, it doesn't mean that I have to get on with his daughter, does it? It's totally unfair, the whole thing. Mum and Patrick are being completely selfish. They'll be moving in with each other next. And then what? Are they expecting me and Lissie to live together too?

Before I know it I'm going to be stuck in the bottom bunk, sharing a bedroom with a cello and a girl who's really up herself. I don't think Mum and Patrick have thought this through at all, because if they had, they'd have finished with each other by now.

I got up and ran downstairs.

'I'm not meeting Patrick's daughter, Mum – not on Friday, Saturday, Sunday or ever.'

'But why?' asked Mum, dripping washing-up

water off the end of her Marigolds as she blinked at me with this horrified look on her face. Good. Now she knew what it felt like to be shocked by something awful.

'Because I don't want to. It's like some kind of grotesque arranged marriage, this! I've got enough friends at school and if I want any more I'll find them myself, thank you.'

I was about to go belting off again when Mum said, 'Well, what about phoning each other or e-mailing or something? I'm sure when you've exchanged a few bits of information about yourselves, you'll be dying to meet each other to see what you both look –'

She'd hit the nail on the head. 'What we look like?' I shouted. 'Well, *she* might be dying to, but I can assure you I won't. So you can tell Patrick that Becca isn't playing, OK?'

And then I *did* storm off, slamming the door so loudly I almost missed Mum's parting words.

'You've got something on your chin, love.'

'I know!' I screamed from the top of the stairs.

3 MY GREAT ACTING CAREER!

I didn't go into assembly because I had to finish copying Louise's history homework. I don't usually crib other people's work (well, at least not all of it), but this time I'd completely forgotten about the history because my mind had been too full of Lissie and spots and boobs and hair for there to be any room left for unimportant things like homework.

Maddy and the others were dying to hear what Mum had said, but I was making them wait till break time, when the history would be out of the way and I'd have time to make a proper announcement. I couldn't wait to see the looks on their faces.

The moment I'd finished copying up the history I rushed to the loos. I was only just in time because they were all coming out of assembly. As my class filed back to the classroom it was easy to join the line, without our form tutor being any the wiser.

'Guess what!' said Maddy, latching on to me instantly. 'We're doing *Oliver!* at the end of term. You know – the musical. It's auditions at lunchtime, but Miss Wightman's already got a good idea of who she thinks will manage the main parts. I'm going for the part of Nancy.'

I didn't think I was in with much of a chance of a decent part in *Oliver!* because of it being the musical version. I'm good at acting, not singing. All the same I thought I'd go along and audition because it would be great if I *did* get a decent part. The only trouble was, nearly all the parts were for boys. And those would probably go to all the year sevens.

But then something suddenly clicked in my mind. If I was in *Oliver!*, I'd have to go to lots of rehearsals. I could even *invent* rehearsals. What a totally perfect excuse for putting off meeting Lissie! *Sorry, Mum, we've got a rehearsal after school and then I've got my homework to do.* It might be pushing my luck a bit, but I reckoned I could make up the odd weekend one as well.

'Are you going to audition for anything, Bex?' Maddy wanted to know.

'What girls' parts are there, apart from Nancy?'

'There's Widow Corney,' said Louise.

'Does she have to sing?'

''Fraid so,' said Maddy.

'What about Bet? That's Nancy's friend,' said Maddy, looking excited.

I must have been looking doubtful.

'My mum thought you were great in *Cinderella*, Bex. And she teaches drama, you know,' said Tanya. And that clinched it. I decided to have a go.

At morning break, the four of us went off to the sports field for the news-breaking ceremony.

'I can't wait another second,' said Maddy, the moment we set foot on the grass.

'OK, get this,' I started, letting my eyes travel slowly from one face to another. 'I've got a stepsister!'

Silence. I wasn't sure that they believed me. Surely they ought to be speaking.

'She's called Lissie and she's thirteen like me,' I gabbled. 'Neither of us knew about the other one because Mum and Patrick weren't certain that they were going to stay together. But now they definitely are.'

'Hey, brilliant!' said Maddy.

'Yeah, that's great,' said the other two. 'Have you met her? What's she like?'

'Right – here comes the bad bit. She's really

good on the cello, she's got long straight dark hair and a lovely face, and she's clever and sensitive.'

I rolled my eyes and finished up going cross-eyed.

'Well, never mind. I bet she's not half as funny as you,' laughed Maddy.

I joined in the laughing, but I didn't really feel like it, because I'd been kind of hoping Maddy might say *But* you're *clever and good-looking, Bex.*

It was obvious why she hadn't – because I *wasn't* clever or good-looking. And if Maddy didn't think I was, then Lissie wouldn't either. Hmm! I was getting more and more screwed up by the second.

It was lunchtime and I was late for the auditions. I just happened to be coming out of the canteen at the same time as Mrs Sherman, the French teacher. She was struggling to get the TV and video along the corridor. They were on a trolley with wheels that weren't rolling properly. She asked me to give her a hand. If I'd known we were going to the other end of the school with the stupid thing I might have thought twice. But I didn't, which was why I was practically the last one in to audition.

I'd passed Maddy on the way and she'd leapt up and down, grinning all over her face because she'd got the part of Nancy. (Surprise, surprise!)

By the time I went into the audition room, Miss Wightman was packing her things away.

'Oh, Becky!' Her eyes widened at the sight of me. I was obviously the last person she'd been expecting. She was probably hoping it would be someone better than me. Like a boy. 'I'm afraid I've cast just about all the parts, Becky . . .'

She must have seen the disappointment in my face. 'Which part were you hoping for, dear?'

'Um . . . Bet?'

'That's gone.'

'Widow Corney?'

'That's gone too.'

'Er . . . what's the name of the housekeeper who looks after Oliver at the nice man's house?'

'Mrs Bedwin. I'm sorry, but that part's gone too. I'm afraid there's a real shortage of girls parts . . . unless . . .'

'Yes?'

She looked as though she'd just had a brilliant idea.

'Well, I *am* looking for someone to play the part of the second old woman. There isn't much to say, but it's quite an . . . interesting part to act.'

An old woman? I'd already got a big enough complex from being an ugly sister. And *second* old woman? Why not go the whole hog and give me the part of Bill Sykes's dog? It looked like my career was taking a nosedive.

'Er . . . is it a big part?'

'Not exactly big – just three appearances – but it's important, because the first old woman is the only person who knows Oliver's real identity, and she confides in the second old woman on her death bed. So it's the second old woman who reveals the truth to everyone.'

Why did I get the feeling she was making it sound better than it really was?

'OK, I'll –'

I was going to say 'I'll think about it', but Miss Wightman clapped her hands together and said, 'That's great, Becky. Jonathan *will* be pleased.'

'Jonathan?'

'Yes, Jonathan Ringmer in year seven. He's playing the part of the first old woman. None of the girls wanted to do it, and I felt Jonathan was a bit too tall to play one of the boys. Also, he'd struggle with all the actions in the songs.' (Her voice turned from grave to bright.) 'He wasn't too sure about playing a female rôle, but the others persuaded him that he'd be great.' (Back to grave.) 'I've been a bit concerned actually, because I wasn't sure if he'd manage it.' (And bright once more.) 'If he's got someone to follow, though, he'll be fine. So I'm delighted. And so will Jonathan be when I tell him.'

She was walking me to the door, nodding and smiling as she talked. I'd got about five seconds to get out of this ghastly situation, because there was no way I was going to act with Jonathan Ringmer. It's not very cool to have any kind of association with kids who are in the year below you at school, but *Jonathan Ringmer* – acting with him would be totally die-worthy.

I bet his so-called 'friends' set him up. I could just imagine them all saying 'Yeah, go on, Jonathan. You'd be great at being an old woman!' Then they'd laugh hysterically behind his back. And poor old Jonathan wouldn't realise they were taking the mickey. He'd just be so pleased that someone was actually paying him a compliment that he'd agree to anything they said. I didn't really know Jonathan, but I'd seen him around and heard a lot about him. Louise's brother is in his class and Louise has told us things that her brother has said about him.

All the year sevens think he's really thick. I don't know if that's true or if it's just that he looks it. He's either got this permanent gormless, vacant look on his face, or he's staring intently at the floor. He's also about fifteen centimetres taller than everyone else in his year, and when he walks his arms don't seem to swing properly, and his legs are all kind of gangly. That makes him terrible at sport. But apparently he does try very hard, so all the teachers like him. It's no wonder he hasn't got any friends, poor thing.

I *did* feel sorry for him, but as for acting with him – forget it! I wasn't the coolest girl in year eight by a long way, so I needed to hang on to all the cred I had, and acting with Jonathan wouldn't be doing me any favours at all.

'Er . . . actually, Miss Wightman . . .' I began. But it was like she was immune to my voice because she opened the door, checked there was no one else waiting and went rushing off gabbling about late lunches. I ran after her. 'Er . . . Miss Wightman, I'm not actually definite about . . .'

She was a fast walker.

'First rehearsal on Friday lunchtime, Becky. See you then.'

I was right. She *was* immune. I'd have to catch her at the end of the day, because no way was I acting with Jonathan Ringmer.

Absolutely no way.

4 THE TIP OF THE ICEBERG

That evening I had a terrible row with Mum. I really yelled at her, telling her she should have thought about me before gallivanting off to Portugal with Patrick, leaving me with the strictest granny in the history of grannies. Mum was furious and finished up by asking me what I expected her to do – dump the man she loved because he happened to have a thirteen-year-old daughter?

It was a horrible argument and I hated the way I was talking to Mum but I just couldn't help it. I bet sweet, sensitive Lissie didn't talk to Patrick like that.

Then right in the middle of ranting and raving something occurred to me. I don't know why I'd never thought about this before. It was so obvious and it made everything a whole lot better instantly. Lissie must live with her mum, and just visit her dad every other weekend or something. So actually, I'd hardly have to see her at all. Even if Mum and Patrick got married, she'd only have to put up with ordinary old me every other weekend, and I could make sure I was out most of the time.

'Lissie lives with her mum, right?' I asked, trying to sound calm but knowing it was coming out bolshie. 'She just visits her dad every other weekend, yeah?'

'No, she lives with Patrick.'

I felt gutted. Things were worse than ever. And then of course, just because I'd asked a question about Lissie, Mum took that to mean

I was getting interested in meeting her.

'Her mum – Patrick's ex-wife – has got a new partner. Well, not exactly new. They've been together for years and have their own two children. Lissie feels more comfortable living with her father. She goes to see her mum every other weekend.'

I didn't speak. Mum must have thought my silence was a good sign because she launched into even more interesting-facts-about-Lissie.

'Lissie finds she can practise her cello better at her dad's, because there's no one to disturb her. Well, I suppose the same applies to homework too. Patrick says she's a bit of a perfectionist.'

It felt like there was a volcano inside me waiting to erupt. We'd got as far as *lovely looking, clever, sweet, sensitive, very musical and a bit of a perfectionist*. And that was probably just the tip of the iceberg. Next thing, Mum would be telling me Lissie represents her school at sport, comes top in everything, is the most popular girl in year eight and owns her own pony.

She was going to be positively thrilled when she met me, wasn't she? She'd have to use her super brain to quickly find a way of never having to see me again. And Mum clearly thought she was the best thing since the invention of the mobile phone. But nobody seemed to care about me and what I thought.

'I'm hoping Lissie's interest in music might spark off an interest in you, Becky. Just imagine – you could play duets together. Your part would have to be much easier than Lissie's, of course . . .'

That's when the volcano finally erupted.

'Oh what bliss!' I screamed, swinging right round to eyeball her. 'And maybe when you and Patrick get married, we could form a lovely family string quartet. Get real, Mum! I don't want to live with the girl. You can't do this to me! It's not fair.'

Mum looked shocked. 'Calm down, Becky.

Who said anything about marriage? Patrick and I simply want to carry on seeing one another, and we both thought it would be nice for you and Lissie to meet each other.' Her voice changed to a pleading tone (new tactics). 'Why don't we arrange one day next week, love? I'm sure once you've met Lissie, you'll wonder what you were worrying about.'

'You just don't get it!' I yelled at her.

Neither Mum nor I spoke for quite a while after that. We both just kept our eyes on the TV screen. Then Mum got up to make some tea.

'Want a cup, Becky?' she asked me in a completely normal voice.

'Yes please,' I said without looking up.

'Oh, and you might like this . . .'

She handed me a piece of paper from her jeans pocket and then went through to the kitchen.

I looked at the paper. On it was written Lissie's e-mail address. I stuffed it into the pocket of my school skirt then watched telly and drank tea for the next hour, but I didn't take in a single thing, because of the discussion that was going on inside my head.

There's no harm in just writing one little e-mail.

What about when she replies?

Write another one. Then you'll find out what she's really like.

And she'll find out what I'm like.

Not necessarily . . . You can pretend to be cooler than you are.

But she'll find out when she meets me.

You don't ever have to meet. Just keep putting it off and putting it off.

I can't do that for ever. Eventually we'll have to meet.

If you've exchanged loads and loads of e-mails, at least you'll know what to expect when you do have to meet her.

OK, I'll give it a whirl.

* * *

I didn't want Mum to think I was dead keen so I made sure I gave a few yawns and then I said I was going to bed.

'OK,' she said. 'Watch the bugs don't bite.'

I just wish she wouldn't say that. It sounds so babyish.

As soon as I got into my room I switched on my computer and went into my e-mail. I typed in Lissie's address, reading it carefully from the bit of paper, then wondered what I should put for 'subject'. I wanted it to be something witty. I thought about it for ages but couldn't think of a single thing, so I left that bit blank and got on with the message.

Half an hour later, after using the delete button a lot, this is what I'd come up with . . .

Hi,
Weird situation this, isn't it? Still, what else can you expect from grown-ups! Typical!

OK, let's get the boring stuff over with – I'm thirteen. My birthday is May 15th. I'm Taurus, I've got fair hair, I'm average height, and right now I'm knackered because I've just finished learning my lines for the school production of Oliver! Sorry – gotta go!

Becca Price.

I felt quite pleased with the final version. I'd spell-checked every single word because my spelling's not all that good, so at least she wouldn't be able to laugh at me about that. And the e-mail had come out sounding much cooler than the real me, so with a bit of luck she might think I was OK.

I read it through one more time, then clicked to send it, and got the shock of my life because that's when I found that Lissie had already written to me!

* * *

Dear Becca,

I'm not even sure if you like being called Becca – my dad didn't know. He said he thought Becky OR Becca, and I think Becca is a lovely name, so I decided to call you that. If you hate it you MUST tell me! It's so weird that my dad and your mum are going out with each other and you and I have never met. I couldn't believe it when Dad told me – especially when he said you were thirteen too. What are your hobbies? And can you tell me what sort of music you like and what films, also your favourite colour and animal? My favourite colour is red and my favourite animal is a monkey. I'm not sure what my favourite film is. I'm supposed to be practising my cello at the moment, but I was so dying to write to you that I've put on a tape of me practising! I've attached a photo of me. Can you send me a photo of you please? Thanks.

Anyway, I'd better go before my dad gets suspicious!
Love from Lissie.

I read through the message twice and then wished I could somehow get mine back and write another one in a completely different way. She sounded quite nice, and she'd even called me Becca, instead of boring Becky or stupid Bex. I'd thought it was best to be cool, but now I realised that was a silly idea. She was going to think that not only was I thick, I was also horrible. And then when she saw my spots, my clumpy hair and my flat chest, she'd hate me more than ever. What a mess!

My hand shook as I opened the attachment. When the picture came up I stared at it for ages. She was smiling but only just – as though she was thinking about something completely different. Her hair was very dark and hung almost down to her shoulders, all shiny and healthy *and all the same length*. And worse, she didn't have a single spot. The photo cut off just below her neck so it was impossible to see if she'd got any boobs. I bet she had though.

I disconnected and flopped back on to my bed. There was no way I could ever meet this girl. She'd think I was hideous. And there was certainly no way I was going to send her my picture. I shut down my computer and went to bed, wishing I'd never gone along with this e-mail idea in the first place.

And as I lay there, I started thinking about what had happened at the end of school. I'd gone to the staffroom to find Miss Wightman, and I'd seen her talking to Jonathan Ringmer. I was about ten metres away, but I heard my name mentioned, and I saw Jonathan smiling and nodding. Miss Wightman patted him on the back and he walked off still grinning to himself. I didn't have the heart to go and say *Sorry, I don't want to be in Oliver!* after that, because I knew Jonathan was banking on me.

Something suddenly clicked inside my head. This whole Jonathan thing was the exact reverse of the whole Lissie thing. *I* was the cool one where Jonathan was concerned. I decided at that moment that however difficult it was, I wasn't going to pull out. It would be hard, putting up with all the mocking and the sniggering, but I was going to try for Jonathan's sake.

5 MAKING SOMETHING
OF MYSELF

On Friday lunchtime, all the students who were needed in the first part of the first act of *Oliver!* waited for Miss Wightman in the main school hall. Maddy wasn't in this part, and neither Louise nor Tanya wanted to be involved, so I was the only one out of my group of friends who was there. Looking round, there were quite a few year eights and nines, but mostly year sevens.

Jonathan was standing on his own by the wall bars. He was reading with a big frown, holding the book close to his face. There was a picture of a motorbike on the front cover. His lips were moving slowly. He must have been saying the words to himself. When Miss Wightman came in, he was the last to notice. She even had to tell him to put his book away, and then he looked up and went red. A few of the other year sevens sniggered and nudged each other.

Here we go! Remember your resolution, Becca.

Miss Wightman told us the *Oliver!* storyline, asked if we'd seen the musical (most of us had) and said we were going to start acting straight away, even though we'd be reading from our scripts.

'Right, Jonathan and Becky, you're the first on, and I really want to see you looking like a couple of poor old women, all bent and wrinkled and slow. We're going to make you up to look very shabby and positively ancient! You don't need a script for this opening section because you've got no lines.'

Everyone laughed when she said that. Jonathan looked at the floor. And that's when I suddenly clicked on that they were actually laughing at me too, so now it was *my* turn to go red. Miss Wightman was still explaining what we had to do.

'Pretend you're bringing on piles of plates and dishing them out on to the tables – we're actually going to use real tables for the performance – and then go off and come back with the spoons.'

Jonathan was still wearing a big frown and he didn't move from the wall bars. I didn't think he'd heard a single word Miss Wightman had said.

'Come on, ring-a-ding! Wakey wakey!' said the boy who was playing the part of Dodger.

Oh dear, this was every bit as bad as I'd thought it was going to be! I must have been mad to have got involved. Jonathan wouldn't have a clue how to act being old and wizened.

Everyone would laugh like mad at us when we went on. I'd just have to get it over with quickly and then surely Miss Wightman would see it was hopeless. I met Jonathan's eyes and jerked my head so he'd follow me. And he did, like a little lamb. No, make that a great big sheep.

'We've got to pretend to be carrying a pile of plates each,' I told him slowly and clearly. 'Put them out on imaginary tables, OK? Then go back for spoons.'

'Spoons, yeah,' said Jonathan. He looked so spaced out, I wasn't sure if he'd taken in what I'd said.

We were at the side of the stage out of view of everyone, so I tried out my toothless old hag look. Jonathan immediately imitated me, and plonked himself right behind me, practically glued to my back as though he didn't dare go any further away in case he missed something.

'Come on,' said Miss Wightman. So I made my legs a bit more bowed, and shakily hobbled into everyone's view, pretending to put plates down. Jonathan was so close behind me I could feel his breath on my neck. We must have looked a right pair of idiots because the entire hall erupted when we appeared. I wasn't sure if they were laughing because Jonathan was doing something funny behind me, or just because they always laughed at Jonathan.

I could feel myself tensing up. I didn't want to be a part of this horrible mocking. The only reason I kept on going was because out of the corner of my eye I could see Miss Wightman watching us with this sort of half-smile on her face. Suddenly I wondered if Jonathan was making funny signs at me behind my back – although surely Miss Wightman would have stopped him if he had been. All the same I had to know, so I kept myself all hunched and bowlegged while I slowly turned round to look at Jonathan. He must have thought he was supposed to do the same thing, because *he* turned round too. Then we were both facing the wrong way.

'Go on,' Miss Wightman called. 'Keep going.' Then she too collapsed in giggles, which made all the kids crease up even more. So by the time we'd put the spoons out, everyone had tears rolling down their faces they were laughing so much.

I couldn't go on. Laughing was bad enough, but this kind of hysterics was too much to put up with. But then I got the shock of my life.

'That is utterly fantastic!' said Miss Wightman. 'This wasn't supposed to be a funny scene at all, but you've made the rôles so much better with that comic interpretation. Well done!' She turned to the others. 'These two have set a very high standard. I hope the rest of you are going to be able to follow it.'

I didn't dare look at anyone, but the laughter had stopped and the atmosphere felt different. I was gobsmacked. We'd done something great without even meaning to! Jonathan was wearing a strange half-smile as if he still wasn't sure whether Miss Wightman had really meant her words of praise or whether she was being sarcastic.

'She thought we were really good, Jonathan,' I said, giving him an encouraging smile.

'It was probably you she meant was good,' he said, hanging his head.

'No, it was both of us. Honestly.' He looked up then, but didn't smile and I don't think he believed me. 'We ought to work out how we're going to do the rest of our scenes. Stay here, I'll get my script.'

When I got back he'd slid down the wall and was sitting waiting for me. I'd no sooner worked out how we were going to do our next bit, and explained it all to Jonathan, who nodded a lot and grinned even more, when Miss Wightman called us and we were on again. This time there were loads of year seven boys on stage with us.

'Right, do it how I said, Jonathan, OK?'

He gave me yet another grin then slowly turned it into a twisted old hag's gormless leer, as he rounded his shoulders and bent his knees. He was really getting into it now – and not just by chance, like he had done the first time. I found myself imitating him, and that's how we made our second appearance, pretending to carry the enormous cauldron of soup for the boys.

'Ready to sing . . .' called Miss Wightman.

But no one could sing a word, because once again they were all doubled up laughing. If I'd been on my own I wouldn't have been able to keep acting with everyone creased up all round me, but Jonathan never batted an eyelid. And that's what made me follow suit.

'You two *are* a couple of pros!' said Miss Wightman, when our scene was finished.

I felt like singing, I was so pleased.

'See you on Monday,' I said to Jonathan, at the end of the rehearsal.

He nodded and went loping off down the corridor on his own.

'So how did it go?' Maddy asked, the moment I joined her and Louise in the classroom. Tanya wasn't there.

'It was good. I've got quite a bit to do at the beginning.'

'Louise's brother says that Jonathan Ringmer is the old woman, but he's not, is he, 'cos you are.'

I'd been a bit worried about this conversation, because I'd never told the others I was acting with Jonathan Ringmer, and I knew they had to find out some time. But now that everyone thought we were so great it didn't seem all that bad any more.

'We're both playing the old hags. You should have seen us! Everyone was killing themselves laughing. We never meant to be funny – it just came out that way when we did it. Jonathan can't help himself. He looks funny without even meaning to.'

'Weird, more like,' said Maddy, rolling her eyes.

They were both staring at me as though I'd completely lost my marbles. They must have thought I'd invented the 'everyone was killing themselves' bit to make up for the awfulness of having to be on stage with Jonathan Ringmer.

'No, he was good – honestly. You can ask your brother, Lou.'

'He's not in it. He just knows how gormless Jonathan Dingbat is,' Louise told me in a flat voice.

'Well, he's not gormless when he's acting. Ask the other year sevens.'

'Good old Bex. Nothing fazes you, does it?' said Maddy, putting her arm round me. 'I wish I could be like that.'

If she only knew! But I couldn't tell my friends how screwed up I felt about Lissie. It was too private.

Most days after school I walk to my gran's house then Mum picks me up when she's finished work. Gran's getting severely on my nerves at the moment because she's always criticising me. This week's topics are clothes and attitude. (My clothes are 'scruffy and shapeless', I'm 'lazy', 'don't make any effort to push myself' and am 'never going to make anything' of myself if I 'carry on like this'!)

'But I *am* making something of myself,' I told her today. 'It's just that you don't happen to like what I'm making.'

'Don't get smart with me, young lady. It won't wash,' she replied.

I didn't have the faintest clue what she was on about. Perhaps I ought to nominate her for the Tyrannical Granny of the Year Award because, I'm telling you, she's in with a fighting chance of winning, the old bag!

She's Dad's mother, and she's got all Dad's

hardness but none of his softness. I only put up with her because if I didn't go to her place after school I'd have to do clubs till Mum could pick me up after her work. There isn't a drama club and I'm not particularly interested in art, netball, rounders or nature. It's great when I get invited back to Maddy's or one of the others', but Mum gets worried about letting me go too often because it's hard for her to have my friends back, except at weekends. So that just leaves Gran. Thank God for *Oliver!* rehearsals! In fact it might be worth making sure I had one every single day (even if I didn't)!

When we got home I helped Mum make Spaghetti Bolognese.

'Have you heard from Lissie at all?' she asked me, trying to sound really casual. But I could tell she was dying to know the answer.

'Uh-huh.'

If she was waiting for me to say anything else, she'd have a long wait.

'And didn't you think she sounded nice?' Mum went on, brightly.

'OK,' I mumbled, tipping the onions I'd just chopped into the pan.

Mum must have decided she was getting nowhere fast because she quickly changed the conversation to school and I told her about the *Oliver!* rehearsal. I tried to demonstrate how Jonathan and I had acted and she laughed just as much as Miss Wightman had done. Then she went and spoilt everything with her next words.

'I don't think Lissie's ever done any acting, you know, Becky. I'm sure she'd be quite impressed if you told her about *Oliver!* It's no different from her cello playing or her Italian, really.'

Maybe Mum was right. I'd even come slightly round to the thought of meeting Lissie after the

Oliver! rehearsal. Then I suddenly realised what she'd just said.

'Italian? What Italian?'

Mum looked a bit flustered. 'Oh, didn't I mention that Lissie has taught herself Italian? It's only because the instructions for her cello music are in Italian, so she got interested in the language and started to teach herself.'

Great! So now she's bilingual. I expect her cello playing is better than Mum's been making out too. My drama seemed pretty pathetic now.

'Don't be silly, Mum. It's not as if I've got the lead rôle. Lissie's probably on about grade seven cello or something. It's hardly the same thing.'

There was a silence – a very loud silence that told me everything.

'She *is*, isn't she?' I said, as I slowly turned to face Mum.

'Is what?' asked Mum, all wide-eyed and innocent.

'Is on grade seven cello.'

'Er . . . I can't remember exactly.'

'Yes you can, Mum. Tell me the truth. Is she or is she not on grade seven?'

'I think that's what Patrick said,' said Mum softly.

Hallelujah! The girl who Mum fondly imagined I would love to have for a stepsister was a genius. Next to her, I would look like the world's biggest moron. Only uglier. Gran was right – I'm never going to make anything of myself.

6 A HOT DATE WITH MR PERSONALITY

I was tucked up in bed, eyes tight closed, but I knew there was no way I'd ever get to sleep unless I checked the stupid thing. I didn't know why I kept thinking about it all the time. It wasn't as though I even *wanted* to hear from Melissa Musician. It would definitely be better all round if I could just forget she existed, but unfortunately I couldn't.

Sighing, I dragged myself out of bed. In fact I kept sighing right up until I'd switched on and connected, and then I gasped, and started reading as fast as I could with big goggle eyes.

Another e-mail. Wonders would never cease!

> *Hi Becca,*
> *At least I know what to call you now!*
> *Wasn't it weird that our e-mails overlapped!*
> *Shows we must be on the same wavelength!*
> *My birthday's on 11th June, by the way, so*
> *you're 27 days older than me. My star sign*
> *is Gemini. Pity. It would have been great*
> *if we'd had the same star signs, wouldn't it?*
> *How tall are you? I'm 1 metre, 55. Don't*
> *forget to answer my questions about your*
> *favourite hobbies and everything. Hope*
> *Oliver is going well. It sounds really cool!*
> *I'd better go now. Please send me your pic.*
> *Love Lissie.*

I read it through twice, feeling more and more
hacked off with every word. I bet Mum and
Patrick talked and schemed about how to get
me to co-operate and meet Lissie. But a much

worse thought had entered my head. What if Lissie was in on their scheming? I could just imagine them talking.

Oh Patrick, get Lissie to say that she thinks it's really cool being in Oliver! *That'll go down well.*

Good idea, Pauline. I'll tell Lissie to drop it into an e-mail.

It had been such a bad idea, this e-mailing. Lissie just made me feel useless at everything. I bet she'd worked out how many days there were between 15th May and 11th June in no time at all. I tried to do it myself, just to see if I could. Somewhere in the back of my mind I was thinking how great it would be if she'd got it wrong and I could correct her. Then she'd think I was quite bright – well, at least at maths. So I started working it out. It took about four goes, because I kept forgetting whether I'd actually counted the 15th as one of the days or not. But in the end I made it 27, so Lissie was right. Big surprise!

I shut down the computer and got into bed, then I lay there staring at the shadows on the curtains and trying to increase my brain power by working out how many days I'd been alive. I don't remember getting past four months, which is 122 days.

'My stepbrother let me ride on the back of his motorbike,' Jonathan suddenly said.

I swung round sharply to look at him. It was Monday lunchtime's rehearsal, and we'd been sitting there in silence for so long, watching the action on the stage, that it came as quite a shock when he started talking to me.

'Your stepbrother? I didn't know you had a stepbrother.'

'That's because you don't know anything about me.'

I thought he was taking the mickey at first, but then I realised he was simply saying what was obvious.

'N-no, you're right – I suppose I don't. So how old is he – your stepbrother?'

'Nineteen. He's nice.'

'Do you live together in the same house?'

'No. He used to come round quite a lot, only now he's older he'd rather do stuff with his mates.'

I found myself staring at Jonathan. I couldn't help it. It's just that he sounded so – so normal. If only the others could forget his size and his funny way of walking and the fact that he didn't click on to stuff very quickly, they'd realise he was OK.

'What did *you* do?' he asked me.

'What?'

'At the weekend?'

'Oh . . . nothing much. Shopping with Mum. Got babysat by my gran – even though I swore I didn't need it – which was torture.'

'Don't you like your gran?'

'These days, I like her about as much as I like slugs.'

Jonathan grinned. 'Be good if she got on the back of my stepbrother's bike and he took her for a burn.'

It was such a weird thing to say. Maybe that was why he wasn't popular with the others, if he came out with stuff like that. I didn't reply, just pretended to be watching the rehearsal, but in my mind I was imagining Gran on the back of this roaring motorbike, clinging to a young bloke in black leather, screeching round bends and wearing this manic grin. It was such a funny picture I laughed out loud.

Jonathan started laughing with me, even though he couldn't have known what was going on in my head.

'What's funny?' I asked him.

'Your gran on the back of my stepbrother's bike,' he answered, staring straight ahead with a big grin on his face.

So he *did* know.

Suddenly I realised that the rehearsal had finished and people were beginning to leave the hall. Quite a few year sevens and eights glanced at Jonathan and me on our own in the corner. I saw two boys from my class nudge each other. Oh great! So now I was going to have to put up with Maddy and the others thinking I was out of my tree. I'd never be able to convince my friends that Jonathan was quite nice underneath.

'We'll do your dying scene next time, you two,' Miss Wightman called across to us. 'As long as you stick to the words in the script, I don't mind if you want to put in your own . . . embellishments, shall we say. I know I can trust you to work out something good.'

She chuckled as she went out and Jonathan and I were left all on our own. I felt very honoured. I'd actually heard one of the year sevens gasp when Miss Wightman said we could do it how we liked. She hadn't said anything like that to anyone else. I looked at the stage.

'Why don't we try out our dying scene right now, Jonathan? It'll be brilliant having the whole hall to ourselves.'

But the bell went, long and loud, and we both had to get back to afternoon registration. Now we wouldn't have a chance to prepare for the next day's rehearsal and it was mega important to my cred that we were really good, because I was pretty sure Maddy was coming to it.

'Look, where do you live, Jonathan?'

'Goddard's Close.'

'That's at the top of the high street, isn't it?' He nodded. 'Well, I live in Rye Street which goes off the high street, so that's not far away at all. Tell me your phone number and I'll give you a ring later so we can arrange to get together.'

It was quite a shock finding Maddy, Tanya and Louise waiting for me outside the hall. I couldn't help going a bit pink because of being with Jonathan.

'See you later,' he called as he went plodding off in true Jonathan style.

'Yeah . . .' I replied brightly.

'Got a hot date with Mr Personality, Bex?' giggled Louise.

I should have told her to shut up and leave him alone because he was really nice when you got to know him. But it was as if my mouth wasn't linked up to my brain.

'Yeah, like I really have!' I said in a horrible hard tone.

'I thought you said Jonathan was all right,' said Maddy.

This was my cue to put things straight. But how could I when I'd just been so sarcastic about him?

'He's OK,' I said, desperately trying to think of a way of changing the conversation.

'You're blushing, Bex,' said Tanya. 'I reckon

you're secretly going out with him.'

'Don't be stupid. It's OK acting with him, but I wouldn't be seen dead with him out of school.'

'Yeah, leave her alone,' said Maddy, putting her arm round me. Then she spoilt it with her next words. 'You *have* gone quite red though, Bex. I hope you're telling us the truth.' She gave me one of those looks a teacher gives you when they're pretending to be cross.

They all laughed, and I knew Maddy was only joking. Little did they know. Meeting Jonathan 'out of school' was exactly what I was going to do.

7 A NEAR MISS!

'I know you're going to be furious . . .' Mum said, the very second we were in the car going home from Gran's.

Red alert! Red alert! I could just feel that this was going to be something really bad.

'Why?' I practically growled.

'OK, I've invited Patrick and Lissie over to have dinner with us this evening.'

She was gripping the steering wheel and staring straight ahead. I wasn't surprised she looked tense. She knew I was about to kill her.

'That's no good. I've arranged to practise

the dying scene with Jonathan.'

Mum looked as though *she* was practising a dying scene, because she let out her breath really slowly in a big sigh. Then she took another deep breath and tried again. 'Well, you'll just have to un-arrange it, won't you?'

'No, I can't. This is the only chance we've got of practising, Mum. We're doing the scene tomorrow. Look, why can't you leave it alone?'

'Because *I* want to see Patrick occasionally in the evening, and *he* wants to see me, but neither of us likes leaving you two on your own. And I know you're not exactly keen on the idea of having Gran round. It just makes sense for all four of us to be together.'

'It might make sense to you, Mum, but it doesn't to me.' *Apart from the bit about Gran, which makes perfect sense.*

Mum smouldered gently all the way home.

One to me, I think!

* * *

I went straight up to my room the moment we got in, then crept halfway down the stairs again and listened. Sure enough, it was only a couple of minutes before I heard Mum on the phone telling Patrick that the evening was 'off'. I heard her sigh and then carry on speaking, *all* in sighs, which made me felt horribly guilty. I turned and went quietly back to my room and lay on the bed thinking everything through.

Maybe it wouldn't be too bad just to meet her once.

Come off it! It would be every bit as bad as you thought, and *more.*

But I can't put it off for ever.

No, but you can put it off for longer than this. *And anyway you really* have *got to practise with Jonathan.*

So I waited till Mum had finished talking to Patrick then I used the phone in her room to ring Jonathan.

'Jonathan's coming round in half an hour,

Mum. Is that all right?' I said, going into the kitchen a few minutes later.

Her sighing mood hadn't left her. Unfortunately. I wished she'd stop doing it. It only made my guilt trip worse.

'I suppose so. Do you want to have a pizza from the freezer?'

'Yeah, that would be great. I'll do it.'

I'd decided upstairs that I was going to be the nicest, most helpful girl I could, to make up for being totally uncooperative about meeting Lissie. The bottom line was, I was just too scared. Mum was making her out to be Super Kid – brains, sensitivity, artistic flair and great looks, all rolled into one.

Even Gran had had a go at me about meeting the girl. I don't know whether Mum told her to, or whether she was just doing it off her own bat. But either way she missed by a mile with her nasty granny lecture.

'I don't know why you're making all this fuss

about meeting a girl of your own age,' she'd said in her tight-lipped voice, with her head wagging about critically. 'She sounds jolly nice, if you ask me. Helps with ironing and cooking and everything.'

I'd nearly asked her if Lissie had also got an old hag for a granny, but I'd been too depressed for sarcasm.

'Do you want a cup of tea, Mum?'

'That would be nice, thanks, Becky.' (Big sigh.)

'Would you like Jonathan and me to work in my room or where?'

'You can work in here if you want. I'll go in the living-room.'

I decided to have a quick shower while I was waiting for the pizza. When I came skipping downstairs ten minutes later, Mum told me that Maddy had just phoned.

'Maddy? What did she want?'

'Nothing – well, just to say that she was popping round.'

'Popping round?' It came out in a breathless squeak because I could feel another big crisis coming up ready to whack me on the head. 'When?'

'Any time now.'

'I hope you didn't say I'd got Jonathan coming, did you?'

'No. Why? What's Jonathan got to do with all this?' She eyed me carefully. 'He *is* an acting partner, not a boyfriend, isn't he?'

'Course he is!' I protested loudly. Then I started wailing and wringing my hands. 'Omigod! What am I going to do? If Maddy sees me with Jonathan, I'll never ever live it down. This is terrible!'

'What on earth are you talking about, Becky? What's wrong with the boy?'

'He's year seven for a start . . .'

'Wow! Big crime!' said Mum sarcastically.

'And he's very tall for his age.'

'Tut tut!' said Mum. (She could be really

aggravating when she wanted to be.)

'And he's kind of . . . vacant, so he's not at all popular.'

'Do you find him vacant?'

'No, I like him. But then he's different with me.'

'And that's because you're nice to him. Pity the others can't take a leaf out of your book.'

I looked at my watch. 'Oh Mum! He'll be here in a minute. They're going to run into each other on the doorstep. What am I going to do?' I squealed.

'Let them run into each other,' said Mum, opening the oven door and wafting away the smoke. 'I think this is ready. I'm fed up with these crispy crusty shop ones. Lissie said she'd give me a recipe for homemade ones. That might be something you could do together one day – make pizzas and hire a video. It would be lovely, wouldn't it?'

If I heard another word about the wonderful

Lissie, I reckoned I'd throw up.

'I don't expect she'll have time in between her cello practice and her Italian, Mum.'

Mum bit her lip. I could tell she regretted what she'd just said.

'Shall I put another pizza in – if we've got Maddy as well as Jonathan?'

'No, I'm going to get rid of Maddy,' I said, opening the front door. 'Jonathan'll be coming from the other direction, so just let him in when he gets here, OK?'

'If that's what you want,' said Mum, in a sickeningly adult way.

I pulled the front door shut behind me and got ready to run, but there was no point. Maddy was getting out of her big sister's car just across the road.

'Hi!' she called, grinning all over her face. 'Gemma was coming this way so I cadged a lift. I was bored at home so I thought I'd come round and see you.'

'Oh. Right.' *Omigod*! Now *what am I going to do*? She was heading for my front door. I had to stop her. 'Actually, it's a bit difficult at the moment because Mum's boyfriend's here . . .'

I was taking shifty glances round Maddy's spiky henna hair, desperately trying not to show that I was looking out for Jonathan coming from the opposite direction. Any second now he'd come lumbering up the road grinning at me, and my cred would be shot to pieces.

Maddy looked puzzled. 'So? Your mum never said anything on the phone . . .'

'No . . . everything was fine when you rang, but now . . .'

'What?'

I blurted out the first thing that came into my head.

'Patrick's a bit – you know, emotional . . .'

'Why? What's the matter? Has your mum dumped him?'

Omigod, there's Jonathan! Coming round the

corner. If Maddy turns round she'll see him. Think of something good, Becca – and fast!

'It's not just that. You see, my new stepsister's here too.'

Maddy looked gobsmacked. 'Your stepsister! Wow! Is this, like, the first time you've met her?'

I nodded and gulped. Jonathan was getting nearer. I had to get rid of Maddy. I didn't have a second to spare. Help! Maddy smiled as though she was genuinely pleased for me.

'I'll tell you all about it tomorrow. She's really amazing, you know!'

'Oh thanks, Bex. Brilliant!'

'I've gotta go now, because she can only stay another ten minutes. So . . . bye!'

Don't turn round, Maddy. Whatever you do, just walk off in the direction you came from.

'The walk'll kill me, you know.' She was grinning and pretending to be old and frail. She must have thought my worried look was because of her. 'Only kidding. Seeya!'

Jonathan was about twenty metres away. I could see him out of the corner of my eye. *Don't call out, Jonathan. Whatever you do, don't call out!*

She finally set off.

'See you tomorrow then, Maddy.'

'Yeah, bye!'

I rushed inside, shut the door and stood shaking in the hall, trying to calm my breathing down. A minute later I nearly jumped out of my skin because the doorbell rang right in my ear hole. I opened it but kept well back.

'Hi!' said Jonathan, grinning at me. I yanked him inside and shut the door quickly. 'I just saw Maddy go,' he said with a bit of a question mark in his voice.

'Yeah, she popped round.' As I turned to take him through to the kitchen I asked him as casually as I could whether Maddy had spoken to him.

'No, she'd never speak to me. She thinks I'm stupid.'

'But did she see you?'

He frowned as though it was a bit of a strange question.

'Dunno. Don't think so.'

So now I had to wait till tomorrow at school to find out whether my cred had been blown to pieces. I also had to tell my friends about the amazing Lissie. At least that bit wouldn't be difficult. I knew enough facts about the wonderful Lissie Raines to keep the whole class entertained for hours.

8 MORE PRESSURE

The moment I walked into the classroom, Maddy swooped down on me, demanding every single detail about my new-found stepsister. Big relief! I reckoned that if she'd had even a nano-suspicion that Jonathan had been at my place, she would have made me suffer.

'Start with her looks,' said Maddy.

It was a relief to tell someone about her at last. It had been horrible keeping all my worries secret – especially from Maddy – but how could I talk about her when I hadn't even met her? And there was no way I could ever have admitted to being such a chicken.

I rolled my eyes to the ceiling. 'She's really nice looking – lovely skin, lovely straight dark hair down to her shoulders.'

'What was she wearing?' asked Louise.

'Jeans and a T-shirt.'

'It's good that she dresses the same as you. Wouldn't it be awful if she was really old fashioned?' said Tanya.

'Yeah, or really ultra trendy with a tongue stud and green hair,' said Maddy.

'But we haven't got much else in common,' I said, getting ready to milk this one. 'She's grade seven cello, is really pretty, and altogether a superbrain.'

'Wow!' said Louise. 'Pity you! Does she make you feel kind of stupid?'

I nodded.

'Poor old Bex,' said Maddy. 'Never mind, I bet she can't act the part of an old hag.'

'How do you know she's really clever?' asked

Tanya. 'She didn't get all her school books out to impress you, did she?'

Maddy pretended to stick her fingers down her throat. 'Oh no! She didn't, did she?'

'No, I already knew she was clever. Not from her – from Mum.'

Maddy was frowning. I could tell her mind was on something else. A moment later her eyes widened as though she'd just remembered something.

'What was up with Patrick, by the way?' she said. 'Your mum *hasn't* dumped him, has she?'

Oh God! I'd forgotten about that. What made people emotional? Well, I cried over Little Women. *That's not enough – reading a book. Maybe writing one . . .*

'He's written this book.'

'Cool! What's it about?'

I looked on the art board for inspiration. There was a picture of a tramp sitting in a doorway with a blanket draped round him.

'It's about down-and-outs – you know people who live on the streets of London.'

'Really? How does he know anything about that?'

Blimey, Maddy. Do you have to know every single detail?

'Er . . . he used to . . . be one.'

If only I could shovel those last five words back into my big mouth! But I couldn't. Anyway it didn't really matter. Maddy would never find out.

After lunch, when it was time for the rehearsal, I deliberately made sure Maddy and I were late because I wanted to be certain that when we turned up at the hall, the others would have gone in. No one's allowed in the hall until the teacher gets there, so everyone hangs around outside. Jonathan was always one of the first there, and he'd be pretty certain to mention something or other about our meeting at my house last night. But if Maddy and I turned up late, we'd be able to go straight into the hall, and Jonathan wouldn't think it was odd if I didn't go over and chat to him. He'd see that I was with Maddy and keep away from us. It's like an unwritten rule: if your friends are around, you stick with your friends.

'Look!' said Maddy, glancing at her watch in horror. 'I don't want to be late for my first rehearsal! Quick, Bex. Hurry up!'

We belted down the corridor. I prayed all the way that everyone would have gone into the hall and my prayer was answered. We went in just in time to hear Miss Wightman asking for Maddy to go up on to the stage.

I clocked where Jonathan was, and made sure I stood as far away as possible. Once Maddy was absorbed in her lines, I risked a quick glance at him. He was looking in my direction. I gave him an only-just smile then looked back at the stage intently to give him the message that I did *not* want him anywhere near me right now.

A minute later I risked another glance and saw that he was looking down at the floor with a really sad expression on his face. I felt like the most horrible person in the world at that moment.

I dragged my eyes back to Maddy, who was singing brilliantly, but I couldn't stop thinking about Jonathan. Goodness knows why! I mean, it's not like it's my duty to look after him, is it? It's not my fault if he hasn't got any friends. I folded my arms and knitted my eyebrows together in a huge effort to concentrate on what was happening on the stage, but my guilty feelings wouldn't go away. Somewhere deep in my heart I knew why, too. Jonathan must have felt as though I was just using him, that I didn't really like him at all. Because if I did, I'd speak to him whether or not my friend was around.

If only Miss Wightman would rehearse our dying scene, then I could be nice to him without

Maddy thinking I was a dur. But there was so much work to do on Maddy's bit, it was obvious we'd never to get to do ours in this rehearsal.

'You were really brilliant, Maddy!' I told her as we walked off together.

'Cheers, Bex,' she answered, putting on a spurt. I could guess why. She wanted to get back to the others so that they could ask how the rehearsal went. Maddy knew she could rely on me to dollop out the praise. I felt guilty again because who did Jonathan have to praise him? And as for people like Lissie – they must go flying through life on cloud nine, plucking their cello strings alongside the angels.

Jonathan had turned off down the year seven corridor. As we passed I took a quick look. A whole crowd of boys were swinging along talking and laughing with each other, ignoring the sad lanky boy with his hands in his pockets and his head down as he lumbered along just behind them. I sighed without letting it show. Why was life so complicated?

That evening I went into my e-mail and found that Lissie had sent me another one.

> *Hi Becca,*
> *I'm sorry we didn't get to meet each other the other day. But it doesn't matter. I know we will soon. You sound like you lead a really busy life! I hope the Oliver rehearsals are going well. Are your friends in it too? What's the name of your best friend? Mine's called Leanne. She's been asking me all about you. I can't wait to get a photo of you then I can tell everyone what you look like.*
> *Please reply soon.*
> *Love Lissie.*

No way was I going to send her a picture now!

I went into the bathroom because the mirror in there makes you look nicer than you really are. Things like spots don't show up. All the same, I still looked horrible. My hair was all greasy for a start and my face was so ugly.

Then I went back into my room and looked at myself sideways in the full-length mirror. I stood up as straight as I could, which automatically made my stomach go in and my chest go out. It was a definite improvement but I couldn't walk round all day like that, could I? I'd get nicknamed Sergeant Major.

I decided to attack my hair with a shampoo for permed or coloured hair which I found in the bathroom. (Not that my hair *was* permed or coloured. I just thought it might do it some good – like magically make it all the same length for a start.) Then I put spot cream all over my face. It stung, so I washed it off and just put tiny dabs on the actual spots. I'd only got two, which wasn't bad for me. (I didn't count the chin one because it was definitely on its way out.) Maybe I could get Mum to take a picture of me in quite a dark place. As long as my hair was washed and you couldn't see my spots, I might look reasonable enough to send a copy to Lissie after all. In the meantime I thought I'd better e-mail her, or she'd think I was a total freak.

> *Dear Lissie,*
> *Thanks for the e-mail. You're certainly right about me being busy. I'll be glad in a way, when this Oliver production is over, but it's good fun doing it, so in another way I'll be sorry. My best friend is called Maddy and she's in the play too. We have a great laugh together. Haven't really got any recent photos of me, but as soon as I get one, I'll send it.*
> *Seeya.*
> *Becca.*

* * *

When I went down to the kitchen I decided to try out my sergeant major look on Mum. She noticed instantly.

'Nice straight back, Becky. You look as though you've been having deportment lessons.'

I couldn't tell whether she thought I was overdoing it or not.

'Does it look stupid walking round with a back as straight as this?'

'No, you look lovely – like a model.'

If only she'd not said those last three words! I knew perfectly well that I looked about as much like a model as I looked like Prince Charles. Now I couldn't believe anything Mum said.

'We've all got to take up-to-date photos of ourselves into school,' I said, casually flipping through the TV guide a moment later. 'It's for this English project. Can you take one of me, Mum? I haven't got any recent ones.'

'I don't even know if we've got a film in the

camera,' she said absent-mindedly.

It didn't take me a minute to find the camera.

'Yes, there is a film in it,' I said, handing it to her.

'Let's wait till tomorrow, shall we? It'll come out much better in daylight.'

'No, let's do it now. I've just washed my hair. What about in the bathroom?'

'The bathroom? Are you mad, Becky? Of all the rooms in the house, you choose the bathroom as the background?'

'I'll stand in front of the door, then the loo won't show.'

She shook her head as though she was despairing of having such an odd daughter, but she followed me upstairs all the same.

'It's not going to come out very well, you know,' she said, leaning back against the bath, the camera to her eye. 'It's far too dark in here.'

'Just take it, Mum. I can't stand here grinning

for another second. My mouth's starting to quiver.'

She lowered the camera. 'I'll take it on one condition.'

Here we go!

'That's blackmail.'

'You don't know what I'm going to say.'

I bet I do.

'What?' I closed my eyes and waited.

'That you meet Patrick and Lissie in town for lunch on Saturday.'

'Look, you know I hate the thought of it. It's not fair.'

'Exactly. You've hit the nail on the head, Becky. I know you hate the *thought* of it. But I'm sure that if you actually *do* it, you'll really enjoy it, and you'll be pleased that you've done it. It'll be a big weight off your mind.'

My head felt like it was the rope in a tug-of-war competition. I kept on nearly giving in, because after all, what was one little lunch? But then I'd suddenly remember how clever and talented and good looking Lissie was, and how much Mum clearly adored her, and I just knew I'd never be able to hack it.

'OK, forget the stupid photo,' I said, rushing out of the bathroom and into my bedroom.

Mum tapped on the door a moment later, as I knew she would. I made sure I had my back to her. 'Sorry, love. I shouldn't have put you under that pressure,' she said. 'I'll take the photo a bit later, and you don't have to meet Lissie until you're ready.'

'What if I'm never ready?' I said, raising my voice as I swung round to eyeball her.

She smiled and didn't reply, which just made me madder than ever for acting like a two-year-old when she was being all nice and kind and adult.

9 MISS POPULARITY

Maddy, Louise, Tanya and I were walking along the corridor at the beginning of morning break, when Jonathan appeared ahead of us.

'Here comes your boyfriend, Bex!' said Louise, just loudly enough for all of us to hear.

The other two giggled. I made a funny noise that was supposed to be a giggle but came out like a mouse squeak. This was exactly what I'd been dreading.

'Hi, Becky,' said Jonathan, as he got nearer.

I heard a stifled giggle come from one of the others. I had precisely one microsecond to decide whether or not to reply. If I did, I'd lose my cool and have to suffer endless taunts. It would start with just the three of them, but in no time at all it would spread round the class. I'd be an outcast. If I didn't reply, I'd probably just make Jonathan a bit upset for a little while. Well, it was obvious what I had to do, wasn't it? I turned my back on Jonathan as he passed us, and said loudly to Louise, 'Did you do the French homework?'

'Not very well,' she replied, but I hardly heard her because from behind us came a loud thud. We all turned round to see Jonathan kick the wall. Hard. My stomach seemed to be on elastic, and my face felt as if all the blood had left it. He was really wild. It could only have been because I'd ignored him.

I didn't know what to do or say – and for once the other three seemed a bit stuck for words too. Then Maddy turned back round and carried on walking, so the rest of us followed suit.

'Looks like your boyfriend has got a bit of a temper,' said Louise.

'Shut up, Louise. He's not my boyfriend, OK.'

'OK, OK!' said Louise, putting her hands up as though to ward off my temper.

Maddy linked her arm through mine, which was a big relief. Then Tanya linked up on the other side, and Louise joined on the end. I'd kept my cred, but a big part of me wished I hadn't.

For the rest of the day I worried about Jonathan. If he didn't calm down he was going to get himself in big trouble. By lunchtime I'd got myself into a really bad state. I considered not even going to the rehearsal – pretending I felt ill or something. But we would be doing our dying scene today, and Miss Wightman wouldn't be very impressed if one of us didn't show up.

Maddy wasn't needed for this rehearsal though, and I'd heard her telling the others that she wasn't going to watch.

'What, in case that big kid starts throwing tantrums or something?' Louise grinned.

I never heard Maddy's answer. All I knew was that I still hated myself for blanking Jonathan like that. I'd never do it again. But how was he going to react towards me?

Within ten seconds of walking into the hall after lunch, I'd got the answer to that one. Miss Wightman was facing Jonathan, her arms folded, head on one side, tight-lipped and very unhappy. Uh-oh!

'What do you mean, you're quitting? You can't just quit when it suits you, Jonathan.'

You could have heard a butterfly landing on the floor, the kids were so tuned in to the drama going on in the middle of the hall. Jonathan didn't speak, but he turned his head slightly when I came in, and a hard look came over his face. Miss Wightman put two and two together.

'I see. So you two have had some kind of argument, have you? Well, you can go and sort it out, then come back when you've decided to stop wasting my time.' She turned to one of the year tens. 'Can you go and find Maddy, please? We'll rehearse one of her songs while we're waiting.'

Jonathan walked out and I stood there not knowing what to do while Miss Wightman talked to the rest of the cast. But then she suddenly broke off what she was saying because she'd spotted that I was still there.

'Go after Jonathan and sort yourselves out,' she said sharply.

So I scurried out like a frightened little animal. As soon as I was in the corridor I broke into a run. Jonathan was walking so slowly he hadn't even turned in to the year seven corridor.

'What's the matter, Jonathan?' I said, when I

drew level with him. (Stupid question, but I had to say something.)

'You know what's the matter,' he growled. 'You're embarrassed to be seen with me. You can't even say hi to me. How do you think that makes me feel?'

At that moment the year ten girl passed us and I saw that a few paces behind her was Maddy.

Jonathan turned away from me. He knew what was coming. And suddenly I saw myself through Jonathan's eyes, and I felt as low as a dung beetle. I didn't care any more what Maddy (or anyone else for that matter) thought.

'Come on, Jonathan,' I said, putting my hand on his arm.

Maddy stopped in her tracks and stared at my hand as though she was fully expecting it to drop off at any moment from having been in contact with Jonathan Ringmer's arm. Then she gave me this really sympathetic look, and mouthed, 'Problems?' I nodded but I didn't move my hand. 'Good luck,' whispered Maddy, then she rushed off behind the year ten girl.

Jonathan must have heard those last two words. He probably took them the wrong way, as though I needed luck to survive being on my own in a corridor with him. I wanted to explain that she didn't mean anything horrible, but he wouldn't have believed me so there was no point. If only I'd just said 'Hi' before.

'Miss Wightman'll be waiting for us,' I said. 'We'd better get on with it.'

'Go without me,' he said, shaking my hand off his arm roughly. 'I don't want to be in it any more.'

That was all. He walked away, and I knew it was pointless to follow him.

When I told Miss Wightman that Jonathan was still refusing to be in the play, she went mad for about thirty seconds, then switched abruptly from hopping mad to action lady.

'Right. Who wants to take Jonathan's place?'

'Me! Me!' called about twenty year sevens.

'We'll try you, Edward Dunbar,' she said briskly. 'Go on stage with Becky now. Do the very first bit of the opening scene. You've seen her and Jonathan doing it enough times. Just have a bash.'

I don't think I've ever felt such a complete wally as I did when I had to appear in front of everyone, including Maddy, with Edward Dunbar glued to my back trying to imitate Jonathan and failing miserably. I'd wanted this – the first time Maddy saw me acting the old woman – to be the best time I'd ever done it, not the worst. Loads of the kids sniggered, but no one actually laughed like they did whenever Jonathan and I rehearsed together. At one point I caught Maddy'e eye. She was standing there with her head tipped on one side and a semi-scornful look in her eyes.

Now she thinks I'm a useless actress. Great!

'It's not really working,' said Miss Wightman, about thirty painful seconds later. 'Goodness knows what we're going to do about this.' She was frowning and tapping her foot on the floor. Then she suddenly stopped and said, 'Anyway, I haven't time to think about that now. Let's get on with the next scene.'

Edward jumped down from the stage, looking totally unbothered. I, on the other hand, came down the steps feeling a bit like a book with all the pages ripped out of it. I didn't want to stay in the hall, because loads of year sevens were staring at me, which proved I must have gone red.

As I wandered back to the classroom I made a quick summary of all the people in my life who were hacked off with me . . .

- Mum (because I refused to meet Lissie)
- Gran (because she always was)
- Patrick (because I was the reason why he couldn't see Mum more often)

- Jonathan (because I was horrible to him in front of my friends)
- Miss Wightman (because I hadn't managed to sort out the problem between Jonathan and me)

So all in all I didn't exactly stand much chance of winning any Miss Popularity competitions, did I?

10 COME BACK, JONATHAN,
ALL IS FORGIVEN!

At the end of school I phoned Gran and told her I had an *Oliver!* rehearsal and that I'd see her at five-thirty. Then I went to Jonathan's classroom, hoping I hadn't missed him. There was no sign of him, and I couldn't risk asking anyone where he was, or they'd take the rip out of him even more. *Your girlfriend was looking for you, Dingbat . . .*

It wasn't till I was off the school premises that I caught sight of him way ahead, all on his own of course. His head was down and he was swinging his bag so it kept bashing into the hedge. I wondered if he was still upset about what I'd done. Surely he would have got over it by now? But then *I* hadn't, so maybe it wasn't so odd after all.

I ran to catch him up, stopping a few paces behind to think what to say. The bag-swinging was much more ferocious from close up and I didn't want to risk getting knocked unconscious or anything.

'Jonathan?'

He stopped walking but didn't turn round. Then he set off again.

Definitely still upset.

'Jonathan, I only want to talk to you . . .'

'What, you mean while none of your friends are around?'

I didn't reply at first. He had every right to be angry. 'Yeah – I'm sorry about that. I just . . . didn't know how they'd react if I was talking to a year seven boy.'

'You're lucky if that's all you've got to worry about.'

We walked along in silence for a bit and I realised that if I asked him about coming back into *Oliver!* again, he'd probably blow a fuse and tell me to bog off. So I tried something else.

'I was going to go into town.'

No answer.

'Do you want to come?'

'Why?'

'We could go to Gino's.'

'Haven't got much money.'

'I'll pay.'

'Why?'

'Dunno. I want to.'

'That's two answers.'

People reckoned Jonathan Ringmer was thick, but he wasn't.

'OK, one answer. Because I want to.'

'Why?'

'Pass.'

I'd done it! The teeniest flicker of a grin appeared on his face. We carried on walking in silence for a while, and then he said, 'What would you do if we were sitting in Gino's and one of your friends came in?'

'Say hello of course. Tell them to come and sit with us.'

'You wouldn't. You'd go and sit at their table and leave me on my own.'

'No, I wouldn't – honestly.'

I really meant it. I hoped I'd never make Jonathan feel rejected again.

'What was Edward Dunbar like?'

'Uh?' His change of conversation threw me off balance.

'Was he better than me?'

'No. He was the pits. It was so embarrassing.' I knew I had to tread carefully. 'Miss Wightman thought he was useless too.'

'So what's she decided to do then?'

'She doesn't know. She's thinking about it.'

His eyebrows were knitted together as though he was trying to solve the problem of world crime before we got to the next lamppost. I was worried in case he actually walked *into* the lamppost.

'She probably doesn't want me any more.'

'I'm sure she does. She was really hacked off to think that the rôles of the two old women might have to go.'

'Why can't she just have one old woman – you?'

I took his arm and pulled him slightly. 'Watch it, Jonathan. You nearly knocked yourself out.'

He didn't care. He repeated his question.

'Two's funnier. You heard how they all laughed. They really liked the way we acted.'

'I wasn't acting. I just did what you did. I never could have done it on my own.'

Now it was my turn to knit my eyebrows. I was trying to work out why on earth Jonathan had gone along to the auditions in the first place, but I didn't want to come straight out with a dodgy question like that, in case he got upset again and refused to come back into *Oliver!*

'Did you actually audition for the part of the old woman?'

'Yeah. Everyone said I'd be good at it. They were all going on about how I'd manage it all right because there wasn't much to say and you didn't have to sing or anything. I didn't really get what was going on – you know, them being all nice and everything – but no one, like, sniggered, so I just thought that for once they'd decided not to take the rip or anything.'

His head went down. 'Then afterwards when I told them I'd got the part, they all fell about laughing and started mimicking what I'd be like as an old woman. So then I felt a complete prat.'

I knew there was more to come, so I kept quiet and waited. 'At the end of school I went to tell Miss Wightman that I wasn't going to be in it, and she told me that she'd got a year eight girl to be the other old woman. I said I'd be no good at it, but she just kept saying I'd be fine because of the year eight girl helping me. I asked her who it was and she said Becky Price, and I knew who you were, because of you being one of Danny's sister's friends. So then I thought maybe it'd be OK, because I'd seen you around and I thought you looked nice – you know, kind . . .'

That was the longest speech I'd ever heard Jonathan make. He was describing so much of what I'd actually felt myself – all that stuff about feeling stupid and having to worry about what other people thought. It was weird, but Jonathan Ringmer and I were in pretty much the same boat.

We were outside Gino's now.

'Fancy a Coke?' I asked him as I pushed open the door.

'OK.' His face looked all blank again. I think that was how he got himself ready to face other people.

Unfortunately I knocked into someone who was standing just inside. She turned round and I recognised her but couldn't think where I'd seen that face before.

'Sorry,' I said.

'That's OK,' she answered.

Then I realised who it was. I don't know how I didn't faint or gasp or anything. I was face to face with Lissie.

11 GINO'S

'Let's get out of here. It's a bit crowded,' I whispered to Jonathan.

He frowned round at the empty tables in the café and then looked back at me, still puzzled. 'There are loads of tables.' He plonked himself down at the nearest one. 'Here's one. See?' He smiled as though he'd done something really clever and he was quite proud of himself. I couldn't drag him away now.

'I'll get the Cokes,' I said.

'Why are you whispering?'

'Er . . . I can't stick people who talk loudly in public places.'

'OK,' he whispered back at me, then he pulled a few coins out of his pocket and thrust them into my hand. 'Is that enough?'

'I expect so.'

While I was waiting to be served I looked around. Standing in front of me were the three girls who'd come in with Lissie. Lissie was saving a table for the others. She was staring at the wall. I followed her gaze. She was looking at a picture with loads of different coloured patterns. I wished I knew what she was thinking. It was weird knowing that I knew who she was, but she had no idea who I was.

'Yes please?' the girl behind the counter bellowed at me. I was in such a world of my own I hadn't even realised it was my turn.

'Two Diet Cokes, please . . .' Maybe Jonathan didn't want Diet Coke. 'Diet or ordinary, Jonathan?'

Oh God! I'd spoken much louder than I'd meant to. I bet she was looking at me. I stopped myself taking a quick peek to check, otherwise our eyes would meet.

'Whatever,' said Jonathan in his loudest whisper.

'Two Diet Cokes, please,' I said again to the girl.

When I reckoned it was safe to look, I threw a quick glance at Lissie's table. Three of them, including Lissie, were all leaning forward looking interested, while the one with her back to me was getting something out of her bag. I found myself staring, and the girl behind the counter had to attract my attention again.

'One pound twenty, please.'

And that was when Jonathan decided to pipe up, 'Can you get me one of those chocolate things, Becky?'

He was stabbing the air to show me which chocolate thing he meant. I didn't care. All I was bothered about was the fact that he'd used my name in a voice that was loud enough for everyone in that café to have heard.

Don't turn round, Becca. Whatever you do, don't turn round.

Our eyes had only met for a second at the door, so I could easily say I didn't recognise her from her picture. But if we looked at each other for any longer than that, and I didn't say anything to her, I'd have a fair bit of explaining to do when we *did* eventually meet. She'd want to know why I hadn't come over and introduced myself when we'd had such a perfect opportunity to meet each other. Well, perfect for *her.* She was surrounded by friends and they all looked pretty cool, whereas I was stuck with a dozy-looking giant. This wasn't the image I wanted to put over at all. Also, I hadn't looked in a mirror since lunchtime. I probably looked awful.

I waited till I was back at the table, sorting

out the money with Jonathan, before I risked another glance at Lissie's table. The other girls were laughing at whatever the one with her back to me was showing them, and Lissie was smiling but I could tell she wasn't as interested as the others. Then like a flashlight her eyes suddenly flicked over in my direction. I don't think I've ever reacted so fast in my life. I leaned forward and started talking maniacally but softly to Jonathan.

'You'll come back into *Oliver!*, yeah, Jonathan? I mean, it'd be great if you did. Miss Wightman'd be ecstatic and so would the rest of the cast. You see the thing is, if we only had one old woman – me – I'd have to play the part sensibly and make her into a poor sad old woman, like she's supposed to be. That's why two old hags is so much better. What do you think?'

'Yeah, OK.'

Just like that! I couldn't believe it! He was gulping his Coke and I could see his Adam's apple moving up and down. It really stuck out and made me stare until he'd downed the very last drop.

'Gotta go, sorry,' he said. 'Just remembered Mum said she wanted me straight back home after school.'

'Oh. Right.'

''Bye then,' said Jonathan, scraping his chair back really loudly.

''Bye. See you tomorrow.'

He went, and I sat there sucking my Coke through a straw. It was a good opportunity to make my cheeks go right in, in case Lissie was watching me at that moment. Then I stopped abruptly because I was choking. I tried to cough without making a noise but I knew I was going red in the face. Maybe I ought to get out of the place quickly. I didn't want someone rushing over and bashing me on the back. That would be about the uncoolest thing that could possibly happen.

Fortunately I managed to recover about five seconds later, and I decided it was a silly idea hanging about in the café. Lissie and her friends might take ages, and anyway I couldn't afford another drink. Also I figured I ought to be getting back to Gran's. She'd probably phone the police or something if I was more than one minute late. It's the kind of thing Gran would do.

I got up and slung my bag over my shoulder, which knocked over the chair I'd been sitting on. Bending down to pick it up I could feel my face going even redder. I prayed no one was watching me, but I don't reckon the prayer was working because I could feel eyes on me. I just had to hope they weren't Lissie's eyes. That would have completely finished me off.

Just as I was about to make for the door, I heard one of the girls on Lissie's table say, 'Omigod! That's our bus, Lissie. Quick!'

There was a big scurrying and scrambling to

grab the right bags and rush to the door, and as they tore past me, one of the bags walloped into my side. I couldn't help an 'Ow!' escaping.

'Sorry,' she said to me. 'Really sorry . . . Are you OK?'

'Yeah, I'm fine. Go . . . quick! You'll miss your bus.'

Then they went and I realised that quite by accident, I'd just had my first conversation with my stepsister.

12 ANOTHER BIG FIX!

It was quite late when I went to check my e-mail that evening. I had the feeling that Lissie would have replied to my last one. While I was waiting for it to connect I closed my eyes and tried to remember exactly how she'd looked in the café. Her face looked younger in real life than it did in the picture, but just as pretty. I think she was the same height as me, but I'd been so gobsmacked at coming across her like that, I hadn't noticed much more about her.

Receiving message 1 of 1. The blue line was filling up. And there it was, just as I'd thought –

another e-mail from Lissie. I noticed she'd only sent it one minute ago!

Dear Becca,

An incredible coincidence happened today. I had to go home with one of my friends (Jo), and we went into Gino's in town because two of our other friends persuaded us to. Anyway, there was this girl in there. She was with her boyfriend and I heard him call her Becky, and I also heard HER call HIM Jonathan. Dad told me that you're acting in Oliver with someone called Jonathan, so I started imagining that it could be you. The only thing was that if it HAD been you, you would have come over and said hello to me, because you would have recognised me from my picture. That's how I knew this girl couldn't be you. But it was quite a coincidence, wasn't it, because of Jonathan as well?

Thanks for your e-mail by the way. Can't wait to get a picture of you. Glad Oliver is going so well. I was wondering if you'd mind if I came with Dad to see it when you do the proper performance. I know that might be quite a way off, so I expect I'll see you before then. Dad told me it's your mum's birthday on Saturday and he said your mum was thinking that maybe all four of us could celebrate together in the evening! That'd be great, wouldn't it?
Please reply ASAP.
Love Lissie.

My heart was banging against my ribs by the time I got to the end of the e-mail. It was just so packed with scary things. I felt guilty because of pretending not to know Lissie in the café, and I also felt very worried about this great get-together that everyone except me wanted. How on earth was I going to get out of that one? It was obvious I wouldn't have fixed up to do anything with my friends on Mum's birthday, and I couldn't use the excuse of an *Oliver!* rehearsal on a Saturday night. But no way could I agree to the idea of the four of us getting together because not only would Lissie be majorly disappointed with such a drippy stepsister, but now I had the extra problem of having to explain why I'd pretended not to know her in the café. How come I spend my entire life trying to work out how to get myself out of big fixes?

The first thing to do was to write back quickly and put her off the idea of Mum's birthday. Maybe I should say that I'd already got my own surprise organised for Mum, and tell Mum the same thing, then work out what the surprise should be later. Yes, that was a good plan. I'd have to mention the café though. She'd think I was weird if I just ignored her big long story about Gino's.

* * *

Dear Lissie,

Thanks for your e-mail. Big coincidence about the girl called Becky in the café with the boy called Jonathan!

About Saturday, I've actually already got a surprise lined up for Mum, so I'm afraid your plan of the four of us getting together won't be possible. Sorry about that.

Love Becca.

I sent the e-mail, thought hard what the surprise could be, couldn't think of anything, then went downstairs to talk to Mum.

'Mum, you know your birthday?'

'Yes, I –'

I thought I'd better speak quickly before she mentioned anything about Patrick and Lissie.

'You know how we always do something together? Well, this year I've got a surprise for you.'

'Oh, that's great, Becky. I love surprises.'

She looked so happy and I had a feeling I knew why. Mum thought I was going to give her the surprise of her life by organising something with Lissie and Patrick, didn't she? Nothing I thought of could ever match up to that. So now she was going to have a horrible surprise instead of a lovely one. Another big mess!

I was dying for lunchtime so that Maddy could see Jonathan and me do our scene. I was sure she'd be impressed with our acting, and change her mind about Jonathan when she saw all the others laughing, and heard Miss Wightman congratulate us.

I was more and more confident that soon everything would be fine. But in lesson four, Maddy suddenly threw up all over her desk, and she had to go to sick bay. Next thing I knew, she'd been sent home. Just my luck! That meant she wouldn't be at the after-school rehearsal either. Great!

The rehearsal went well. The moment we finished our scene a great cheer went up. Miss Wightman went completely over the top praising us and patting us on the back. You could see she was really relieved that the comic touch wouldn't have to go.

After we came down from the stage quite a few of the year seven boys clustered round us. One of them asked me if I was thinking of being an actress when I grew up. I felt warm inside because he thought I might be good enough. Then one of the coolest boys said, 'Jonno'd make a good actor too, wouldn't he?' And all the others agreed. I could tell they weren't being sarcastic, but Jonathan eyed them suspiciously as though he couldn't believe this turnaround.

I grinned at him and slapped him on the back.

'You'd be a great actor, Jonathan, because you've got guts. You don't care about being an old woman – you just get on with it. I can't think of any other boy who'd dare to do that.' I looked round at the year sevens to make sure they got my meaning loud and clear. A few of them looked a bit embarrassed.

'Yeah, really daring,' the cool boy agreed.

And then this year ten boy, who was playing the part of Bill Sykes, came up to us. The year sevens stopped talking and looked down. He was supposed to be the hardest boy in the school and if you walked past him in the corridor, you made sure you didn't look at him, in case he said *Oi! What you staring at?* My heart was beating faster because I wondered why he'd come over. Then I nearly fainted when he high-fived first Jonathan and then me.

The year seven boys watched wide-eyed and open-mouthed as he walked away. Jonathan was staring at his hand as though it had been touched by a famous person.

If only Maddy could have seen that.

13 WHISPERING IN
THE WINGS

Miss Wightman was in her strictest mood. It was obvious she was stressed about something, because she was insisting on complete silence the whole time. You weren't even allowed to breathe. Jonathan and I were crouched in the wings waiting for our next entry. Out of the blue he suddenly whispered to me, 'Are your mum and dad divorced?'

I nodded and frowned, putting a finger to my lips to get him to shut up, partly because I didn't want Miss Wightman telling us off, but mainly because I didn't like this topic of conversation.

'Do you see your dad?'

I shook my head. I did *not* want to talk about my dad. I never saw him these days and that suited me fine.

'I don't see mine either,' whispered Jonathan.

'Why not?' I couldn't help asking.

'Because he doesn't want to see me.' I gave him a sympathetic look, but told him we'd better be quiet. He ignored that. 'Why don't you see *your* dad?'

'Same reason as you,' I mumbled.

'Why doesn't he want to see you?'

I wished Jonathan would put a sock in it. It was bad enough even thinking about Dad, let alone talking about him. I was still very angry because he'd had an affair with a woman called Felicity, and left Mum for her. Then they had a baby boy called Zac, and ever since the baby was born Dad seems to find it too much trouble to see me. Mum hated his guts from the moment he walked out on her, and I felt really sorry for her. The baby thing finished me off. End of story. I can't forgive Dad for what he did to Mum, and I don't know if I ever will.

'Why doesn't he want to see you?' Jonathan said again, only his voice was gentler this time, as though he'd realised I was upset about it all.

'He's got a new partner and a new baby, and I'm part of his old life, that's why,' I snapped.

'Same here,' said Jonathan, still whispering. 'But my stepbrother is brilliant. He makes up for my dad.'

I was beginning to feel curious. 'Is that the one who lets you ride on his motorbike?'

Jonathan nodded. 'Have you got any other stepbrothers or stepsisters?'

Suddenly I felt like telling him. Jonathan seemed to understand feelings like mine. It was like I said – we had a fair amount in common.

'I've – I've got a sort of stepsister . . .'

'Yeah? What's her name?'

'Lissie. Only . . .'

'How old is she?'

'Thirteen.'

'Same as you. D'you get on really well? Does she kind of make up for your dad, like my stepbrother does?'

Suddenly I felt stupid. It was ridiculous that I'd never met her. Jonathan wouldn't think I was mad though. His mind didn't work like that.

'The thing is, I . . . er . . . haven't actually met her yet. Only e-mailed her.'

'Why?'

His nosiness was suddenly getting on my nerves. OK, so he was a good actor, a nice boy and he knew what it was like to be teased and mocked and have the mickey taken out of him. But he'd never understand how impossible it was for me to meet Lissie.

'Because I don't want to,' I snapped. 'She speaks Italian and plays the cello like a genius and she's dead clever.'

'You're saying you don't think you're as good as she is, so you don't want to meet her?'

'Yes! OK? Satisfied?'

He screwed up his face as though he didn't get wherever I was coming from.

It was time for our entrance. I nudged Jonathan and we stood up and got into our positions. This was our last scene, where Jonathan had to die. Miss Wightman had made this scene much longer and more important with quite a few lines for me. Jonathan had to cough a lot as though he was dying of consumption. For once we didn't have to be funny. It was a genuinely sad scene. We'd worked out how we were going to do it and we'd practised it pretty thoroughly. All the same I was scared people would laugh at us, because they were used to us being funny. It would ruin it for me if they did.

When we first appeared I waited for the laughter to break out, but none did. In fact it was so quiet I took a quick glance to see if everyone had left the hall. *They're sure to laugh when we start speaking in our old cracked voices*, I thought. But no one made a murmur. We got right through to the end of our scene, with Jonathan pretending to be dead while I hobbled away, head down, as if wiping away my tears. I'd got all the way into the wings and still no one was saying anything. There must be something wrong. I tiptoed down from the stage to see Miss Wightman furiously scribbling on her script. Jonathan got up and as he did, everyone burst into applause. Miss Wightman stopped writing and joined in the clapping.

'Well,' she said, looking from one to the other of us, 'you've done it again!' It looked like she'd got a tear in her eye, but she was being brisk and businesslike to cover it up. 'The problem I've got now, is that I know the audience will want to see more of you, so I've just written in half another short scene. I'll finish it off this afternoon and if you come to the staffroom at the end of the day I'll give it to you, so you can practise it over the weekend.'

I couldn't believe my ears! Jonathan and I walked off down the corridor together, discussing when and where we should meet to practise.

'Give me your phone number,' he said. 'You'll have to write it down because I can't remember numbers.'

He handed me a very chewed biro and I felt in my pocket to see if I'd got anything to write on. I was in luck. The bit of paper with Lissie's e-mail address on it was still there. I scribbled my number on the back of it and handed it to Jonathan.

'Well done, Jonno,' said a couple of year sevens as they passed us.

Jonathan stared after them, waiting for the

sarcastic laughter. But it never came.

'See you outside the staffroom at the end of school then,' I said.

'Yeah seeya!'

14 SET-UP

On Saturday morning I took Mum breakfast in bed.

'*Happy birthday to you!*' I sang chirpily as I carried the tray into her room. 'Here's your present.'

She sat up, yawning, and said, 'This is a nice surprise.' But I could tell she wasn't half as happy as she was pretending to be. I guessed she'd found out from Patrick that my great birthday treat couldn't possibly be anything to do with him and Lissie as they didn't know anything about it.

'I wonder what it is?' she said, shaking the parcel, then smelling it and trying to feel it through the wrapping. We'd played this kind of game since I was a little girl. It was a sort of tradition and Mum was trying her best to keep it up. But it was obvious her heart wasn't in it.

I was glad that at least I'd got her a really nice present. I'd been into town after school before going to Gran's, and bought her some beautiful earrings that I'd been saving up for for ages.

'Oh, these are exquisite, Becky!' She seemed genuinely happy, thank goodness. 'I'll wear them for my birthday treat,' she added. 'I can't imagine what it is.'

She was looking at me in an enquiring sort of way, but as I hadn't actually decided on the surprise I couldn't even give her a clue. I just said 'Ha ha!' with a secretive look on my face, and then left her to eat her breakfast, while I did some serious thinking in my room.

After about ten minutes of getting absolutely nowhere, the phone rang.

'Is that Becky?'

'Oh! Hi, Jonathan.'

'Do you want to practise?'

Clearly Jonathan didn't go in for friendly chit-chat.

'Er . . . yeah, OK. When?'

'Ten o'clock.'

I was quite taken aback. I hadn't expected him to be so organised.

'Yes, all right. Where?'

'Your house.'

I nearly laughed. It was just so funny the way he'd got it all planned.

'See you at ten then,' I said.

All the time we were practising, Jonathan kept looking at his watch.

'Jonathan, have you got a plane to catch?'

He went a bit pink. 'What d'you say that for?'

'Because you keep looking at your watch.'

'Well, you see, I'm meeting my stepbrother at Gino's at half-past eleven.'

'Oh. Right.'

That explained it. I thought his excitement was really sweet.

'Do you want to meet him?' he asked me. I hesitated. 'Only he wants to meet you.'

'Oh, OK then.'

So after we'd practised our new scene we set off down the high street. Mum was going to meet Patrick somewhere or other. I wondered what Lissie was doing. She was probably still at a sleepover with one of her many friends. Or otherwise she'd be practising her cello so hard that she wouldn't even notice whether her dad was there or not. What it must be like to be a genius!

On the way to Gino's Jonathan and I were both quiet. I was planning Mum's birthday surprise. I was going to make her a really nice meal with her favourite pudding, hire her favourite film from the video shop and buy her some anemones, which were her favourite flowers.

The trouble was, the more I thought about it, the more I realised that I was being selfish and horrible keeping Mum away from Patrick on her birthday. And then my guilt turned to anger. It wasn't fair that I was being made to feel bad like this. I never asked for a stepsister.

'I don't think he's here yet.'

'What?'

I'd been so wrapped up in my thoughts I hadn't noticed we'd reached Gino's. Jonathan opened the door and I nearly had a heart attack. There, sitting on her own at a table in the corner, was Lissie.

She stood up when she saw me and Jonathan, and I realised with another shock that she was staring at us with a sort of shaky smile on her face, just as though she was expecting us.

'Sorry, Becky,' said Jonathan. 'I've got to go now. I'm going to meet my stepbrother.'

'What? What do you mean?' I hissed at him. 'You can't leave me here all on my own.'

'You're not on your own. You've got your stepsister.'

And with that he left. I stared after him dumbfounded as I realised what had happened. Jonathan Ringmer – that slow-thinking geek (*not*) from year seven – had somehow set me up. He was going to get killed on Monday!

Suddenly Lissie was standing right beside me.

'I got you a Diet Coke. That's what Jonathan said you'd want,' she said softly.

Still in a state of shock I found myself following her to the table and sitting down. It was a good job there was a chair right there because my knees were about to give way. I didn't know what to say. I was stuck in the middle of my worst nightmare. I hadn't put any make-up on, I was wearing my oldest pair of jeans and my hair was a mess.

'H-how did Jonathan manage to . . .?'

'He e-mailed me. My e-mail address was on the back of a bit of paper you'd given him with your number on it. This was the message.'

She handed me a piece of paper and I read it.

> *Dear Lissie,*
> *You dont know me and I dont know you. Im writing because Becky your stepsister, is my frend. Your e-mail address was on the back of a bit of paper she gave me with her phone number on it. She doesn't know Im writing to you. I wanted you to know that she told me shes not meeting you because your two good for her. Its making her really sad. If you dont want to meet her, reply to this and tell me. But if you do, I can arange it. I hope you do because she is really nice. I did'nt used to have any frends,*

but now everyone likes me all because of her.

From Jonathan Ringmer.

I could hardly swallow, the lump in my throat was so big. I just wanted to cry, but I had to struggle to stop the tears in my eyes from showing because of Lissie. I didn't know what to say. But then she spoke.

'I burst into tears when I read it.'

'Why?'

'Because I felt so terrible.'

'Why?'

(She must have thought I was a complete idiot with a vocabulary of one word.)

'Because I must have somehow given you the impression that I thought I was something wonderful. And I'd never do that, because I'm not, and I'd never think that about me. I'm the least cool person in the whole world. And when I got your first e-mail I thought you'd never want me for a stepsister, because you sounded so much more grown up than me. And I was right, you didn't want me, because you saw me in here, didn't you? And you must have recognised me from the photo, but you still didn't say anything, not even when you e-mailed. And I knew why – it's because you look so much more sophisticated than me. I've been trying to make my hair look like yours instead of hanging in a straight line.'

She looked so sad, I had to come clean.

'But I hate my hair! And when I saw you in the photo with your lovely straight shiny hair and no spots I thought you'd think I looked horrible – and I can't play the cello or anything . . .'

'But I can't act – and I *have* got spots. Look! I just picked the photo that showed them least.'

'But Mum says you're really good at cooking and you speak Italian . . .'

'I've only learnt a few words because I needed them for music. And when your mum was there I cooked the only thing I know how to cook – and that's pizza.'

'But you're really clever . . .'

'The only thing I think I'm any good at is cello – honestly. I came bottom in history and next to bottom in geography. I can't bear to think that you thought all this about me.'

She had tears in her eyes.

'Don't cry,' I said instinctively.

'I won't if you don't,' she replied.

I hadn't realised I'd still got tears in my own eyes.

We were staring at each other through our watery eyes, and at the very same moment we both suddenly saw the funny side of the whole thing, and Lissie giggled. Immediately I laughed, and then we both cracked up.

'This is ridiculous!' I spluttered.

'I know!' she said.

After that we talked and talked about everything under the sun. I even told her I'd been worrying about not having any boobs, and she said she'd been worrying about exactly the same thing, so it turned out that neither of us had anything to worry about! About twenty minutes later I suddenly had the most brilliant brainwave.

'You know it's Mum's birthday today?' I began.

'Yes, I was just thinking that,' said Lissie.

'We could give her the best surprise ever.'

'I was thinking *that*, too!'

We sat there for another whole hour, and it only took about two minutes to work out the plan for that night. The rest of the time we were finding out every single thing about each other. It turned out that the girls I'd seen her with in the café before were her main friends, but she always felt like the one on the outside of the group. The girl she caught the bus with was called Jo. Lissie had been invited to go to Jo's house until her dad could pick her up at six-thirty after work. She didn't often go to her friends' houses though. Normally she just went home, except Fridays when it was Music Club and Thursdays when she had her cello lesson. When she said that I got really excited and in no time at all we were plotting about spending Mondays, Tuesdays and Wednesdays after school together.

I couldn't believe how lovely my new stepsister was, and best of all I couldn't believe how much she liked me. It didn't matter what I was wearing or that I hadn't washed my hair. If anyone had told me an hour ago that in one hour's time I would be arranging to spend as much time as possible with my new stepsister, I would never, ever have believed them.

'We must thank Jonathan,' said Lissie. 'Isn't he a brilliant friend?'

And that was another weird thing!
An hour ago I was going to kill him!

15 SECRETS, SUCCESS AND SISTERS

We decided to bring Patrick in on the secret, because we needed him to book the restaurant and order the taxi for Mum and me. I phoned Lissie at six o'clock when Mum was safely in the bath, and Lissie said that Patrick had been completely bowled over and couldn't believe what had happened.

At seven o'clock, when Mum and I were all dressed up, the doorbell rang.

'Our taxi awaits,' I told her grandly.

She looked utterly bewildered and slightly anxious.

'Are you sure I don't need anything apart from my handbag?' she asked me.

'Quite sure.'

When we stopped outside the Italian restaurant, Mum gave me a big smile.

'This is lovely,' she said to me. But her voice was a giveaway. I knew she was wishing that Patrick could be there. Never mind. Any second now . . .

I opened the door for Mum to go in and she shrieked with delight.

'Patrick! What . . .?' He got up and I just waited long enough to see them hug each other.

'Shan't be a sec,' I said, and slipped back outside again to meet Lissie.

She'd been waiting in the bus shelter across the road, as we'd arranged, and now came rushing over. We were grinning at each other like a pair of little kids. I was so excited.

'Do I look all right?' I asked Lissie anxiously.

We were both wearing black trousers. I had a

purple top with black writing on it and Lissie had a pink top. We'd planned to dress in the same sort of clothes, but I was worried that Lissie looked about a million times better than I did.

'You look great,' she said warmly. 'I bet I look really young and stupid next to you.'

'No, you look brilliant – honestly.'

We opened the door and went in. Mum and Patrick were deep in conversation and it wasn't till Lissie and I were standing side by side at the table, big grins all over our faces, that Mum looked up. I'll never forget the way she just stared at us as though we'd sprouted wings. Her eyes blinked and blinked as they flicked from me to Lissie and back. And then she burst into tears!

'What's the matter?' I asked her anxiously.

'I'm just so happy,' she said through her tears. 'This is the best present ever! I had no idea . . .' She narrowed her eyes and turned to Patrick.

'Did *you* know about this?' she asked him, pretending to be cross.

'Not until a few hours ago,' he said, palms up to show his innocence.

'We only met each other this morning,' said Lissie.

Mum gasped. 'Come on, sit down and tell me all about it. I want every single detail.'

'Would you like to move to your reserved table now?' said the waitress, appearing suddenly.

'Didn't you think that was clever, Mum – thinking of sitting down at a table for three, so you wouldn't guess right up till the last moment?'

'A stroke of genius!' laughed Mum. 'Who thought of that?'

'Becca,' said Lissie.

It was lovely to hear her call me Becca. She was the only person who did.

At seven-thirty two Saturdays later I was in the wings with Jonathan. The curtains were closed and the audience were talking because the house lights were still up. Jonathan and I had found the tiniest gap between the curtain and the side of the stage, and we were peering at the audience through it.

'I can see Lissie,' said Jonathan, his eye to the gap just above my head. 'So that must be your mum's boyfriend on the other side of your mum?'

'That's Patrick, yes.'

The sight of the three of them sitting together like that made me suddenly feel really nervous. I shivered as the lights went down and the audience became silent. On the other side of the stage I could see Maddy sitting on her own reading through her script. She looked up when the house lights went down and our eyes met for a second. She gave me a big thumbs up and I gave her one back. Then she gave one to Jonathan and I thought how funny it was the way things had changed.

The first time she'd seen Jonathan and me do our scene she'd stared open-mouthed and then laughed loudly with everyone else. I'd felt proud at that moment. Then when we'd done the dying scene she'd come up to us both with tears in her eyes and said we were brilliant. Afterwards in the classroom she'd told Louise and Tanya that the scenes with Jonathan and me were the best parts of the whole play.

'You've got to get tickets,' she'd instructed them. 'You won't believe how good Bex is.'

'Can we sit with your mum and Patrick and Lissie?' Louise had asked.

I'd felt a tiny stab of jealousy that they'd be sitting next to my new stepsister. I couldn't help worrying that Lissie might like them better than me, but I knew that was silly. 'Yes, of course,' I said.

Let them find out what a lovely stepsister I had!

'We're on,' Jonathan whispered to me. And from that moment I forgot all about myself and concentrated on becoming one part of a pair of wizened old hags.

We'd made this entrance so many times, and every time we'd got a laugh, but never had the laughter been as loud as now. Inside I was dancing, but on the outside I never stopped being an old woman – not for one single second. And neither did Jonathan. I could feel his concentration behind me, seeping through to me.

The audience brought the whole play to life. They made every one of us act out of our skins and as I hobbled off, hunched and lonely when we'd done the dying scene, I even heard someone sob near the back.

At the end when Jonathan and I took our bow everyone stood up, and the clapping became deafening. I looked for Lissie and when our eyes met she started clapping over her head and jumping up and down.

When we'd got changed and taken off our

layers of make-up, Jonathan, Maddy and I went out to the audience together to join our families. Jonathan's parents and his stepbrother were talking to Mum and Patrick. Lissie, Louise and Tanya were looking out for me and Maddy. The moment we appeared, Lissie came flying over and gave me a big hug.

'You were so fantastic,' she said. 'I was really proud of you.'

Then Louise and Tanya came running up, and Maddy went off to bring her parents over to meet Patrick, and we stood round together, everyone going on and on about how great the show had been.

After a few minutes, when there happened to be a moment of silence, Maddy suddenly turned to Patrick and said, 'Bex was telling me about your book – all about homeless people. And I was wondering if I could have your autograph, please?'

I wanted to shrink into a little ball and roll

away out of sight as fast as possible. I could feel my cheeks burning. Patrick was looking completely puzzled and so was Mum. But Lissie came to my rescue, even though she'd no idea what was going on. She'd just seen how embarrassed I was. I'd explain it all to her once we got away. She moved forwards so she had her back to the rest of us and was practically nose to nose with her dad.

'Stop being so modest, Dad. Give Maddy your autograph.'

She must have been frantically signalling to him to play along, because he suddenly broke into a smile and said, 'Certainly, Maddy. Have you got any paper?'

'Patrick used to be a tramp, you know,' Maddy whispered to her mum just loudly enough for everyone to hear.

Mum coughed and turned round. I could see her shoulders shaking and I knew she was trying to hide her laughter. As soon as Patrick had signed the inside of Maddy's chewing-gum wrapper, everyone started to leave the hall.

I spotted Jonathan on his way out.

''Bye, Jonathan! Have a great weekend!' I called after him.

But he didn't even hear me because he was too busy fastening up his crash helmet and chatting with his stepbrother.

'See you on Monday,' Maddy called out. ''Bye Bex! 'Bye, Lissie!'

Maddy's mum was looking anxiously at Lissie. She knew she didn't recognise her from our school and she must have been wondering who she was.

'Can we give you a lift anywhere, dear?' she said.

'No, it's OK, she's with us,' said Mum.

'Oh, I'm sorry, I didn't realise.'

'I'm Becca's sister,' said Lissie.

A lovely glow spread through me and I saw Mum squeeze Patrick's hand as they smiled at each other. Then an even bigger glow seemed to fill my whole body because I spotted what was on the fourth finger of Mum's left hand.

'Look!' I hissed at Lissie, nudging her and nodding my head very unsubtly at Mum's hand.

'You've got engaged!' screeched Lissie. 'We really *are* sisters!'

And she grabbed both my hands and we started dancing round the hall. Mum leaned her head against Patrick's shoulder and said, 'I told you there was nothing to worry about.'

And that was when I realised that Lissie had been just as worried as me all along. If only I'd known that.

'I do like happy endings,' said Miss Wightman, looking up from sweeping the stage.

'And somehow I think your next rôle might be a touch more glamorous than your last one,' added Patrick.

Lissie and I stopped dancing round and stared at him, while we worked out what he meant.

About three seconds later we broke into our mad gallop once more, only this time we were chanting, 'We're going to be bridesmaids! We're going to be bridesmaids!'

'You lucky things!' said Maddy.

You're not kidding! I thought.

What happens next in the step-chain?

Meet Ed in

GET ME OUT OF HERE

1 NOISE POLLUTION

I don't know how much longer I can put up with the twins and their 'pretends'. They make up such rubbish, and right now they're spouting it just outside my bedroom door, which is getting badly on my nerves.

'Pretend I'm the train driver and whenever we stop you have to get off . . .'

'Yes, and when I get off, I click my fingers and a taxi comes along and I tell the taxi driver where I want to go . . .'

'Yes, and I'll quickly change into the taxi driver.'

'Yes, and you do the click because I can't.'

'I can't either.'

'*I* know! Pretend we're in a special place where they don't do clicks with their fingers. They do them with their tongues, like this . . . *click click click (giggle) click click . . .*'

Oh God, this is driving me nutty! I'll have to tell them to shut up in a minute.

They were getting on some kind of weird six-year-old high, making loud train noises and doing high-pitched screams because they can't whistle. I blocked my ears because I know from experience that once my stepsisters get going, they don't stop till they've gone right over the top. I turned my radio up, but it didn't block out the whistling, giggling, screaming train outside my door.

Finally I snapped, opened the door and yelled, 'Shut up, you two!'

'Shut up yourself, Ed!'

I think that was Lucy. It's hard to tell the

difference between Lucy's and Amy's voices.

'Yeah, shut up yourself, Eddy Teddy!'

One of them giggled.

'Yeah, Eddy teddy bear, big fat pear!'

Massive explosion of laughter from both of them.

'Ha ha! Very funny indeed if you've got a brain the size of a pin head.'

I doubt they heard that. They were both giggling hysterically. I slammed my door so they'd know there was no point in coming back at me with any more witty six-year-old stuff.

The whole house seemed to shake. I'm sure it's going to collapse one of these days. It's very old and pretty big. But not big enough for eight people. And that's how many of us there are.

In the playroom, which is below my bedroom, I could hear Harry bawling his eyes out.

'What's the matter, hmm?' Emma's sing-song voice came floating up.

I bet I know. My two-year-old half-brother is

obsessed with this one particular toy. It's called Reggae Rattlesnake (I'm sure I never had any cool toys like that when I was his age. Life's a bummer!) and it's made of green and yellow coloured plastic and looks about as much like a rattlesnake as I look like Father Christmas. But still, there you go. The problem is that the on/off switch is a bit stiff for Harry and it really makes him mad when he can't work it.

Well, whaddya know! Emma's switched on Reggae. Bet I can guess what's coming next. Harry may have a problem with the on/off switch, but he sure knows where the volume control is. Any second now... Yup! He's switched it right round to top volume. So now the stupid piece of modern technology is snaking round the room, its tongue whipping in and out, while it plays this nerdy pop song with a clunky beat. Reggae might be one neat toy but the noise doesn't half get on your nerves, blasting up through the floorboards.

I turned my radio up to try to block it out. But nothing would block out what came next.

It's impossible to describe the *Omigod-I've-just-seen-a-spider* scream of my stepsister, Alice. Compared with Alice's scream, rattlesnakes and two-year-olds crying seem as soft as a mouse snoring. The scream is her trademark. She does it about fifty times a day – because, like I said, this is an old house, so spiders like to live here. I don't expect they find it quite so great once they've heard that bloodcurdling racket though. They probably turn to each other and say, *Quick, let's get out of here, guys. We've* only *picked a house with a monster living in it.*

'Ed! Where are you? Get this spider out of my room!'

At your service, ma'am.

I sighed, got up and made my way to Alice's room. I've learnt from bitter experience that there's no point in pretending I haven't heard her, because that girl is capable of yelling and screaming for up to an hour, and I'm the only person in this madhouse who doesn't mind picking spiders up (apart from Dad, and he's hardly ever here 'cos he's always at work).

Alice was cowering on top of her chest of drawers. 'It's gone under the bed now,' she wailed. 'You'll have to move the bed. I won't be able to sleep in here tonight if I think there's a spider under there.'

I gave her a withering look. She goes through this kind of spiel every time I move the stupid bed, which is about five times a week in spider season.

The poor old spider tried to run back into the darkness as its hiding place started moving, but I grabbed it like a professional spider catcher, and held it not too tightly in my fist.

'Ugh! Chuck it out of the window!' she yelled, pressing herself against the wall.

And that's when I suddenly thought, *Ed, you sucker. What does Alice ever do for* you?

'Listen, Alice, it's time you got over this spider thing of yours.'

'I can't. I'm too scared. Don't bring it anywhere near me, Ed or I'll scream the place down!' (I believed her.)

'It's a poor defenceless spider, Alice. What's it going to do to you?'

'It's not that. Even looking at it makes me shudder.'

'But if you stop shuddering and think, you'll realise that you're being stupid, won't you?'

'You're the stupid one for arguing about it when it would be much easier just to get rid of it.'

For a ten-year-old she's got a lot of quick answers. And that wound me up even more. I think it was the way she sat there cowering and still giving me orders. I mean, I could have found a nice fat hairy spider and put it down her back. That would have been the quickest way to cure her of her spider phobia. Most of my mates'd do that to their sisters just for a laugh. Alice is lucky to have such a nice stepbrother as me.

'Look, Alice, just hold it. It's not like it's a big one or anything.'

'Mum!' she screeched. 'Ed's bullying me. Come here, quick! Mum!'

Good job the spider had got my hand round it to protect it, otherwise the poor thing would've keeled over from the noise pollution.

'Shut up, Alice. You're frightening it to death. Just try looking at it, then.'

I swear I only took one step towards her – OK, my fingers were uncurling, but very slowly – and she jumped off the chest like a power-crazed grasshopper and landed in a kind of heap on the floor, clutching her ankle and screaming, 'You've made me break my ankle now!'

And that's when Emma – my stepmum, Alice's real mum – came in. She didn't look worried – just kind of frazzled and a bit tatty, same as normal. She'd tied her hair back in one of those big clip things but it was coming loose and bits of it were falling over her face. Harry was on her hip, wriggling to get off. Whenever I think of Emma I picture her exactly like this.

She bent down to let Harry off, then started stroking Alice's ankle absent-mindedly.

'I had to jump off the chest of drawers. Ed was going to put a spider on me,' Alice told her, sobbing dramatically.

'That's cr– ubbish,' I said.

'Ed was going to say a rude word, Mum.'

Emma opened her mouth to speak but Alice got in first again with her high-pitched whine.

'Where is it now, Ed? You'd better not have let it go in here!'

I opened the window and chucked it out. 'There you go! Another one bites the dust,' I said, rubbing my hands. 'I'm going to ring the RSPCA about you, Alice, and report you for psychologically damaging innocent spiders, then making them risk their lives dropping from a second-storey window.'

Now the spider was safely out of the way, Alice made a miraculous recovery. She un-crumpled herself and stood up. 'It's not RSPCA, actually Ed, because spiders aren't animals, they're insects. It's RSPC*I*, except there isn't such a thing.'

She was giving me one of her smug looks with her chin sticking up, which gets to me almost as much as that scream of hers.

'Spiders are arachnids, not insects,' I told her calmly as I went out. 'So it *is* RSPCA.'

I saw Emma trying to hide a smile.

'Your ankle seems to be better now, Alice,' she quickly changed the subject. 'Come down with me and Harry. There aren't any spiders in the playroom.'

'Aren't you going to tell Ed off?' came Alice's sulky voice.

I didn't hear the answer to that because the sound of the phone ringing blotted it out. I went through to Emma and Dad's room and picked it up. We've got three portable phones in the house but we're always losing them.

'It's Tom.' (Tom never bothers with anything like 'hello'.)

'Hiya, Tom,' I said, grinning. I can't help grinning when I'm talking to my mate Tom.

'I'm in town.'

'Yeah?'

'Yeah.'

Phone chats with Tom crease me up. It was obvious he'd phoned to see if I could meet him in town, but he can't quite ask things directly.

'Have a medal!' I said, trying not to laugh out loud.

'What are *you* doing?'

'Not a lot.'

There was a long pause. This was even worse than Tom's usual telephone style.

'I'm in Our Price.'

'Oh, right.'

'Seeya then.'

I rang off and thought about the phone call. It was just as though someone was holding Tom at gunpoint and stopping him from saying what he wanted. I decided to go and meet him. Anything to get out of this place.

Collect the links in the step-chain . . .

 1. To see her dad Sarah has to stay with the woman who wrecked her family. Will she do it? Find out in *One Mum Too Many!*

 2. Ollie thinks a holiday with girls will be a nightmare. And it is, because he's fallen for his stepsister. Can it get any worse? Find out in *You Can't Fancy Your Stepsister*

3. Lissie's half-sister is a spoilt brat, but her mum thinks she's adorable. Can Lissie make her see what's really going on? Find out in *She's No Angel*

5. Ed's stepsisters are getting seriously on his nerves. Should he go and live with his mum? Find out in *Get Me Out Of Here*

6. Hannah and Rachel are stepsisters. They're also best friends. What will happen to them if their parents split up? Find out in *Parents Behaving Badly*